Ghosts of War Smoke

War Smoke is busier than usual as gamblers come to the sprawling town from all four corners of the Wild West to take part in the biggest poker game ever to be staged at the famed Longhorn saloon.

Yet amidst the bustle, and unknown to Marshal Matt Fallen, there are others assembling in War Smoke who have less than honest intentions. As well as hired gunmen and tricksters, Gentleman Joe Laker, famed for his skills as a poker player and his prowess with guns, is also riding towards the town.

As War Smoke swells with unknown faces, another rider is on his way there too, with something far more blood-chilling on his mind than playing cards. As the town's clock ticks down to the start of the big game, Matt Fallen is embroiled in a bloodbath and must fight for his very life.

Ghosts of War Smoke

Michael D. George

A Black Horse Western

ROBERT HALE · LONDON

ISBN 978-0-7198-1630-7

Robert Hale Limited
Clerkenwell House
Clerkenwell Green
London EC1R 0HT

www.halebooks.com

Typeset by
Derek Doyle & Associates, Shaw Heath
Printed and bound in Great Britain by
CPI Antony Rowe, Chippenham and Eastbourne

Dedicated to Dennis

PROLOGUE

Travis Grey was a young man who, it was said, had never truly smiled until he had killed his first victim at the tender age of thirteen. All it had taken was a broken bottle and a festering hatred to achieve this sordid goal. Before all the life had expired from his victim's body the young Grey had stripped him of his gun and belt before he obtained his first stolen horse.

It had been claimed that the murder was a mindless act, yet even in the most damaged of brains there is usually some reason for outrageous acts. The man who had been killed had been one of those who used their strength and power over the seemingly weak and helpless. He thought he had authority over the thirteen-year-old but he had not even conceived that it is never wise to push even the littlest of people too far. For when humiliation boils over into murderous hatred, the results are always the same.

The demons strike back. There is no consideration for their own safety. They do not weigh up the odds of success or failure. They just strike like cornered rattlers.

Behind most murderous acts there is usually a deep-rooted reason. One which makes perfect sense to those with imperfect minds. The sadness of it, though, is that once Pandora's box has been opened, it can never truly be closed again.

The thirst for blood can never be quenched.

Travis Grey had killed his tormentor on that day long ago and had lost more than his innocence in the process. He had also lost his mind and he continued to seek out fresh victims wherever he could find them. Like so many in the lawless West Grey left nothing but corpses in his wake.

A long ride through several states and territories had only added to his ruthless tally. Grey seemed deliberately to head towards trouble, as though something drew him there and he was helpless to do anything but obey his inner demons. No man had ever managed to get the better of the young killer since that fateful day when he had chosen to submit to the evil that, it is said, haunts all men.

Travis Grey began to believe that he was more than just a deranged young gunman. He believed that he had the power over life and death, and in his twisted brain that made him more than just an ordinary man.

It made him invincible.

He cared little for the blood money his vicious acts had brought him over the years. His only desire was to achieve the feeling that inflicting death always gave him. He wanted to experience the strange excitement of his first murder again and again but as with all things they can only truly be savoured once.

Every killing since that day had become little more than a pale imitation of that first act of murderous rage. But, even so, Grey kept adding to the notches on his gun grip as he sought to rekindle the morbid satisfaction he was convinced that he could repeat.

Countless men had paid for his deadly services in the years since he had thrust the broken glass into his first victim. They knew he would always kill his prey to oblige his paymasters. What they did not understand was that Grey would kill just for the pleasure it brought him.

Travis Grey had arrived in the small town of Red Rim only an hour earlier. He had not had time to do anything apart from quenching his thirst at the nearest cantina.

The small whitewashed adobe was filled with equal numbers of Stetsons and sombreros as the painfully thin killer rested his wrists upon the wet bar counter and ordered his first beer. It did not take long before the crowded tavern soon started to buzz with the muffled voices of those who recognized that they had a killer in their midst.

For there was no one who looked more like a killer than the young Travis Grey. Every fibre of his being seemed silently to suggest that he was a gunman. As warm beer quenched his dry throat his audience muttered excitedly amongst themselves of the fight they knew would soon take place.

Wade Provine was somewhere between thirty and forty years of age. He had chosen to remain in the tiny border town because it was a place where men of his sort felt big.

Provine had never really been an outlaw of merit. His only claim to fame had been established no further afield than this small town, where he was a big fish in a small pond.

He was a bully and there was not a man in Red Rim who had the courage to stand up to him. The whispers concerning the newly arrived young stranger soon wafted from the cantina and reached his ears. Provine determined to humiliate yet another in a long line of victims, as he always did. Fuelled by cheap liquor the wide-girthed Provine marched through the curtain of swaying beads and stood staring at the silent Grey.

The sight of Grey's youthfulness encouraged Provine. For the profession of the fresh-faced young killer had not yet had time to mark his features.

To the unknowing eyes of the bullish Provine, the young man was just another of the many naive drifters who regularly stood by the bar. He spat a lump of goo at the floor between himself and Grey and shouted.

'You're standing in my spot, little boy,' he bellowed.

Travis Grey lowered his head and glanced over his broad shoulder at the brute who stood before

11

the swaying beads. He raised the beer glass to his lips and took a sip.

'Don't you ignore me, boy,' Provine wailed loudly. He strode across the cantina to where the stranger was standing. 'I don't like snot-nosed kids that ignore me.'

Travis Grey noticed the fearful faces of the onlookers as they backed away from the bar counter and pressed their backs up against the cantina's whitewashed walls.

'You don't say,' he remarked. He rested his glass on the wet surface of the counter and tilted his head to look at the owner of the loud voice.

'I do say,' Provine roared even more loudly. He came to stand beside the young man who was wearing crossed gunbelts around his hips. 'What you gonna do about it, sonny? You're still standing in my spot.'

Grey straightened up and looked intently at the burly man who was leaning into him. He sighed, then backed gracefully away from Provine.

'Stand there if you've a mind to,' Grey drawled, pointing at the floor. 'You said it's your spot. Take it.'

Provine stepped forward. His belly pushed Grey back even further. A hideous smile etched itself across Provine's face.

'That's my spot you're standing on, boy,' he taunted, pointing at the floor.

'Seems to me like you can't make up your mind, old-timer.' Immediately Grey saw the effect his words had upon his aggressor.

Angrily, Provine raised a hand and was about to poke a finger into Grey's chest when he heard the sound of leather being slapped. The gun barrel felt cold as it pressed into the bully's throat. He suddenly went silent as he heard the gun's hammer being cocked.

'Give me a good reason why I shouldn't kill you?' Grey said in a cold tone. 'Just one reason will do.'

Provine tried to swallow but the barrel of the Colt was pressed so hard against his Adam's apple that it was impossible. Sweat trickled down his unshaven face as he stared into Grey's emotion-less eyes.

'I reckon the cat must have got your tongue, old-timer,' Grey said. Slowly he lowered his gun and slid it back into its holster.

The cantina erupted with laughter. Provine had never seen so many teeth aimed in his direction and he did not like it one bit. The large man stepped backwards and glared through his bushy eyebrows at the youngster, who still showed no sign of emotion.

'Nobody makes fun of Wade Provine, kid,' he snarled angrily, shaking a fist at the younger man.

'I made fun of Wade Provine,' Grey said. 'You best get used to it. I might do it again.'

Provine rested a hand on his gun grip. He hesitated as he recalled how fast the youngster's gun had been drawn.

'I oughta kill you,' he growled.

'Having thoughts about how fast I am with my guns, Provine?' Grey asked. He downed the last of his beer from the handled beer glass.

Provine nodded his head. 'Yep. I don't fancy getting myself filled with lead before I can clear my holster.'

Travis Grey shrugged. 'I'm a gambling man. I'll make you an offer, old-timer. I'll let you draw that hogleg and I won't go for my guns.'

The older man looked at Grey curiously. 'You won't?'

'Nope, I won't,' Grey answered. He held the glass in both his hands and stared at the froth floating on the beer inside. 'But I'll kill you.'

Each man stared at the other.

'I draw my gun and you don't?' Provine repeated the proposition. 'And you'll kill me?'

Grey nodded. 'I surely will.'

Provine grinned widely. 'You'll kill me even though you won't use either of them guns?'

Travis Grey looked blandly at the older man.

'That's the deal. Are you man enough to try your luck?'

'Damn right I am!' Provine shouted. He grabbed his gun and drew it from its holster. His thumb cocked its hammer. As his finger curled around its hammer Grey smashed the glass against the bar counter and thrust its jagged edge into Provine's face.

The six-shooter blasted into the floor.

Blood splattered from the deep wounds as Grey mercilessly slashed Provine's throat again and again. A chorus of gasps filled the room as horrified onlookers watched the sheer savagery.

Grey raised his right boot and forcefully kicked Provine across the cantina into the wall. As the blood-soaked outlaw slid down to the floor a scarlet smear of death marked his descent.

Travis Grey tossed the gore-covered glass at the body as a pool of crimson spread out around the mortal remains of Wade Provine. He then pulled one of his guns from its holster and fired a lethal bullet into the crimson mask that hid Provine's features. The skull shattered, splattering gore across the already bloody wall.

Grey smiled at the sight, holstered his gun and turned back to the bar.

He placed his hands on the counter and glared at the terrified faces watching him. His eyes then focused on the bartender.

'Beer,' he demanded. 'I'm still thirsty.'

The dumbfounded bartender poured a fresh glass full of beer from a barrel on top of the counter. He nervously placed it down between the young Grey's hands and nodded nervously.

'On the house, f-friend,' he stammered.

Grey lifted the glass, took a sip of the warm beer, then stared into the bartender's face.

'How far is it to War Smoke, barkeep?' he asked.

'Ten miles or so,' the bartender replied. 'Why? You intending going there?'

Travis Grey took another swig of beer. 'I was considering it.'

The bartender leaned across the counter.

'They got themselves a mighty tough marshal there,' he warned. 'Toughest critter ever to wear a tin star, I'm told.'

Grey nodded. 'That's what I heard.'

At that very moment the beaded curtain parted and a large man wearing a sheriff's star marched into the cantina. Before he had time to utter a single word Travis Grey swung around, drew a six-shooter and fired. The lawman's chest exploded as he was knocked off his feet and crashed on to the ground. The brief smile that had covered Grey's face soon disappeared as the deadly killer felt the elation of his deed subside in his heartless soul. He twirled the smoking six-shooter on his finger and holstered it.

The killer looked at the horrified faces around the cantina and addressed a question to each and every one of them.

'Is there any more law in Red Rim?'

A wide-eyed Mexican removed his battered old sombrero and shook his head.

'No, *señor*,' he answered shakily.

Grey turned back to the bartender. He glared at the terrified man and curled his finger. 'Come here, friend.'

The bartender ventured forward. His heart was pounding inside his sweat-soaked shirt.

'Can I help you?' he stammered.

Grey nodded. 'What's the name of the marshal over in War Smoke?'

'Why, his name's Fallen,' the bartender replied. 'Matt Fallen. I hear he's faster than spit with his gun. They do say he's taller than a tree and twice as ornery.'

The devilish smile returned to Travis Grey's face as he absorbed the description of the lawman. He placed the palms of his hands on the damp counter.

'Taller than a tree, huh?' Grey repeated the statement. 'I like that.'

'How come?' the nervous bartender asked.

'Trees can be chopped down, friend,' Grey told him with a smirk.

The bartender nodded in agreement. 'I reckon so.'

Travis Grey pointed at the barrel perched on the bar counter.

'I reckon I'll have me another beer, barkeep,' he said, then added, 'Before I go and cut me some lumber.'

The bartender nodded.

ONE

The dust-covered stagecoach was only an hour late as its six-horse team drew the long vehicle into Front Street and headed slowly towards the depot. The driver sat upon his high perch with a boot on the brake pole and the hefty leathers in his experienced hands. A shotgun guard rested beside him with his trusty double-barrelled weapon laid across his lap. It had been a long journey across the range south of the sprawling settlement but at one of the regular stops at a way station both men had gathered a lot of information.

It was valuable news and the dusty stagecoach crew knew that the marshal might be interested in learning of it.

As the stagecoach slowed to a halt outside the depot situated next to a large livery the door of the marshal's office opposite opened and the tall, broad-shouldered lawman stepped into the brilliant sunlight.

Matt Fallen placed his Stetson upon his dark hair and watched the coach as its crew slowly descended from the driver's board to the dusty ground. The guard handed two canvas bags to the disembarking passengers whilst his partner made his way across the street towards Fallen.

The driver had a small package tucked under his arm and walked stiffly over to the lawman.

'Howdy, Matt,' the driver said. He weaved his way between two saddle horses and stepped up on to the boardwalk. 'I got a parcel for you.'

'Much obliged, Rex.' Fallen accepted the parcel and briefly looked at its markings. 'How many passengers have you brought to War Smoke?'

'Two dude gamblers, that's all,' Rex James answered. He poked a pipe-stem into his bearded mouth and fumbled for a match. 'They look harmless enough. You know the sort, Matt, all frilly shirts and pressed pants.'

'Good. They sound like greenhorns to me.'

Fallen watched the pair of well-dressed men step down from the coach, collect their luggage and wander back along Front Street in search of either a gambling hall or a hotel. 'Reckon they'll be gone in a couple of days once they've been parted from their money.'

'Yep. Once the cardsharps get their hands on them they'll be darn eager to high-tail it.' Jones scratched a match down the wooden porch upright and ignited his tobacco-filled pipe bowl. 'They sure look like dudes for the plucking.'

'Did they travel together?' Fallen wondered. He was watching the men talking to one another as they moved into the crowded throng. 'Or did they meet up on the journey?'

Jones thought for a moment before answering. 'Come to think about it, they did join the stage together. They bought two one-way tickets back in Vinegar Junction.'

Matt Fallen rubbed his solid jaw as he considered the information. He started to turn back towards his open office door, then he paused and looked at the bearded driver.

'Got any other gossip I might find interesting, Rex?' he asked.

Jones nodded and a pile of dust fell from his

21

hat and shoulders on to the boardwalk.

'I sure have. Me and Cody heard us a heap of news on our way here, Matt.' He nodded. 'Kinda suspicious news.'

'Well, spit it out, Rex.' Fallen rested a boot on a hitching rail and watched as smoke billowed from the stagecoach driver's mouth. 'I'm waiting.'

'Back at Indian Wells we heard a couple of *hombres* talking over a bottle of whiskey,' Jones began. 'They was saying something about heading to War Smoke to earn themselves a hundred bucks each. Easy money they called it.'

Fallen frowned. 'Two hundred bucks is a lot of money for a couple of drifters to earn in these parts, Rex. Leastways it's a lot of money to earn honestly.'

Rex Jones nodded and pulled the pipe from between his teeth. 'That's what I said to Cody. That ain't honest money they're coming here to earn.'

Fallen eased closer to the stagecoach driver. 'Any idea what the job is that these two drifters are undertaking to do, Rex?'

'Gotta be murder.' Jones puffed. 'Only killing folks could bring that kinda price tag.'

'Yeah, it is a lot of money for honest work,'

22

Fallen said, and sighed.

'That's what me and Cody reckoned.'

The marshal nodded. 'The question is, who they're being paid to kill and who happens to be doing the hiring.'

Smoke encircled Rex Jones's battered old hat as his wrinkled eyes noticed the concern and curiosity etched upon the lawman's face.

'Who indeed,' he agreed.

'What did these two drifters look like, Rex?' Fallen asked curiously. 'How will I recognize them?'

'They looked ordinary enough, Matt,' Jones replied thoughtfully. 'I didn't think either of the critters looked like killers, but you never can tell in these parts.'

'That's true.' Fallen sighed again.

The guard wandered across the busy street with his shotgun over his shoulder. Like his partner he was almost white with trail dust.

'Are you still bending the marshal's ear, Rex?' Cody Barker asked. He scooped some water out of the trough and splashed it over his face. 'He's bin bending my ear for the last eighty miles, Marshal. Come on, Rex. Quit gabbing. We gotta see the depot manager.'

Jones looked at Barker. 'Remember them *hombres* we overheard in the Indian Wells way station, Cody? Was there anything special about them?'

'They just looked like drifters to me.' Barker dried his face on the back of his sleeve. 'Mind you, one of them had himself a real handsome horse.'

Jones slapped his thigh. 'That's right, Matt. One of them was riding himself a black roan. Black as night with two white stockings that went clean past its shoulders.'

'A black roan.' Fallen repeated the words thoughtfully. 'I ain't seen one of them in four or five years.'

'Seemed odd to me, Matt,' Barker observed. 'A drifter riding a real handsome horse like that. Just seemed odd.'

Marshal Fallen nodded. 'Much obliged, boys. You heading on out after you've had some vittles?'

'Nope,' Barker said cheerfully. 'We're finished until noon tomorrow.'

The marshal touched his hat brim as both the men walked back towards the depot office. He tapped the small package that he held between his hands, then turned and walked back into his own office.

He removed his Stetson and placed it on the hatstand. Then he sat behind his desk and opened the parcel. He heard the sound of familiar footsteps entering the office.

'Howdy, Elmer,' he said without looking up.

'Now how did you know it was me, Marshal Fallen?'

'Your boots squeak,' Fallen said.

'What ya got there, Marshal Fallen?' Deputy Elmer Hook's distinctive voice filled the office as his lean figure wandered to the stove. 'It wouldn't happen to be love letters, would it?'

Fallen looked up at Elmer. 'It's just a new batch of Wanted circulars.'

Elmer looked disappointed. 'Now ain't that just a crying shame? You'd think that with you being one of the few unhitched folks in War Smoke the females would be sending you notes all the time.'

'Did you just come here to annoy me, Elmer?' Fallen spread the posters over his desk and began to look through them.

'I come to make you some fresh coffee.' Elmer opened the lid of the blackened pot and peered inside it. 'I was figuring on trying out a new recipe.'

'For coffee?' Fallen raised his eyebrows.

Elmer turned and leaned over the desk. 'Sure enough. I was talking to one of the Chinese down at the laundry and he reckoned his people put special herbs and suchlike in their coffee. He done give me a bag of it. I thought I'd try it out on you.'

Fallen exhaled and shook his head. 'It ain't got gunpowder in it, has it, Elmer? You know what happened when you put that pinch of black powder in that coffee pot, don't you?'

Elmer looked offended. 'It weren't this coffee pot, Marshal Fallen.'

'It wasn't?'

'No, it wasn't.' Elmer shuffled back to the stove. 'That was the other coffee pot. You remember, Marshal Fallen. The one that blew up and knocked the window out.'

Fallen rose back to his full imposing height. 'No time for coffee right now, Elmer. We have to make our afternoon rounds of the town.'

Elmer disappointedly placed the coffee pot back on top of the stove. He adjusted his suspenders and shook his head.

'Sometimes I reckon you just don't like my coffee, Marshal Fallen,' he said with a heavy sigh.

'No wonder you don't get love letters.'

Matt Fallen grabbed his hat and placed it on his head. He was about to leave the office with his deputy when he noticed that Elmer was not wearing his gun. He pointed and the deputy looked innocently down.

'What you looking at, Marshal Fallen?'

'Where's your gun, Elmer?' the marshal asked. 'Did you forget to put it on again?'

Elmer looked down, then grinned coyly. 'Shucks, Marshal Fallen. I didn't forget it. My ma said she was gonna polish the belt for me.'

Fallen grabbed his deputy and hustled him out of the office.

'We'll call in on your ma, Elmer,' he said as he locked the door. 'With any luck she ain't decided to wash your gun in carbolic as well.'

The two lawmen had only just crossed the wide street when the marshal stopped. Elmer could see that Fallen was watching two drifters as they rode into War Smoke. Both riders were as white as a bride's frock, caked as they were in the dust of countless miles of trail, which made them unrecognizable.

'What's wrong, Marshal Fallen?' he wondered. 'You look like you just seen a ghost.'

27

Matt Fallen continued to watch the two dust-caked riders as they continued along Front Street then stopped at the first saloon.

'Not ghost, Elmer. Ghosts,' he corrected. His eyes were fixed upon one of the drifters' horses. It was a black roan with white stockings that went clean up to its shoulders.

'They ain't ghosts, Marshal Fallen.' Elmer chuckled. 'That's just trail dust covering them drifters from head to foot. Fancy you reckoning them varmints was ghosts.'

Marshal Fallen sighed. 'Reckon you're right, Elmer.'

Both drifters dismounted and looped their reins around the hitching pole outside the Dixie saloon. They pulled their rifles from their saddles and ambled up the steps into the drinking hole.

'C'mon, Marshal Fallen,' Elmer urged. 'We gotta do our rounds so I can get back and rustle up that coffee you're looking forward to.'

Matt Fallen rubbed his jaw and followed his deputy down the street. After every few strides the tall lawman glanced back over his broad shoulder at the handsome black roan.

TWO

Apart from their tailored apparel there was little remotely similar about Asa and Olin Fenton. One was dark-haired whilst his brother was blond. Yet they moved as one, as though joined by some invisible force. To everyone who glanced at them the siblings appeared merely to be gamblers. This was something that they neither admitted nor denied, but the truth could not have been more different. However, in a town full to overflowing with gamblers of all varieties neither of the Fenton brothers attracted a second look.

What the onlookers did not know was that the Fenton boys were the deadliest of all killers. They were cold-blooded hired gunmen. They never questioned the spineless paymasters who hired them. All they wanted was the money. If their price was met they would kill anyone and not one accusing finger would ever be pointed in their direction.

Most murders were committed by people with motives. Folks who held a grudge killed the majority of people who ended up in funeral parlours, but some were destroyed by the lust for money. The Fenton brothers did not even know the folks they killed. They killed simply for the blood money and hid behind the guise of motiveless gamblers.

Asa and Olin had honed their skills until they had become two of the highest-paid killers in the Wild West. The two travelled quietly and never drew attention to themselves. In each settlement they visited they added to their personal fortune and at least one more grave to the local Boot Hill.

The seemingly harmless cardsharps took it in turns to play poker while leaving the other to go about their true profession. For five years the Fenton brothers had travelled on riverboats and visited dozens of notorious towns using their simple guise as mere gamblers to conceal their lethal activities.

Had anyone been privy to their purposes they

might have noticed that in each of the places where they had briefly stayed a dead body was soon discovered in their wake. Each victim had been killed with precision and expertise. By the time the unfortunate victim was found the brothers were usually long gone.

Asa and Olin Fenton had never been suspected of any of their crimes and that was what made them so dangerous and valuable to those who hired them. It appeared that they could slip out of any situation unnoticed, like ghosts.

Hired killers came in many shapes and forms throughout the West. Most gunfighters liked to display their prowess like a rooster in a hen-house. Flamboyant attire and well-notched gun grips were frequently seen, but people seldom gave two innocent-looking gamblers a second glance.

All towns west of the Pecos River had gambling houses but War Smoke had more than most. Every town had its fair share of gamblers but War Smoke seemed to be drowning in them. The quietly spoken Fenton boys blended right in to the bustling throng sporting silk shirts and lace ties who had arrived before them.

As was their ritual the unassuming pair wandered down the busy boardwalks with their hat brims pulled down over their brows. They headed straight towards the hotel that, they had been told, would have a room awaiting their arrival.

Asa stopped and pointed up at the freshly painted façade above the porch.

'The Diamond Pin Hotel,' he read aloud.

'This is it, Asa.' Olin nodded. 'Looks a whole lot better than some of the others we've passed.'

The brothers entered the hotel and moved across the lobby to the desk. They noticed that all the soft chairs in the hotel's foyer were filled with men and women dressed in their finery.

They also noticed that a small figure wearing horn-rimmed glasses was watching their approach with a smile that might have spooked most folks. The clerk greeted them with a mouthful of store-bought teeth and turned the register round for them to sign.

The Fentons stopped beside the desk, lowered their canvas bags on to the carpet as the excited clerk clasped his hands in glee.

'Greetings,' he gushed in a tone seldom heard from men in most towns. 'Welcome to the Diamond Pin. It's so nice having new faces in our hotel.'

Olin touched his brim. 'Howdy.'

'We've got a room booked here,' Asa added.

The clerk seemed even more excited.

'What would the names be, gents?'

'Fenton,' Olin said. He pulled a long slim cigar case from his breast pocket and opened it. He withdrew a cheroot and put it between his teeth.

While Olin trimmed his cigar the clerk, nodding his head, found the information he was seeking in the large ledger.

'Fenton,' he said. 'Asa and Olin Fenton. You have a suite and it is fully paid for up until the eighteenth.'

'Two weeks?' Olin raised an eyebrow as he looked towards his sibling. 'Our friend is looking after us, Asa.'

The clerk scratched a match and raised its flame to the cigar in Olin's mouth. Olin sucked in smoke and nodded his gratitude.

The clerk blew the match out. 'Are you boys here for the big poker game?' he enquired.

'What big game?' Olin asked through a cloud of smoke.

'The Longhorn saloon has the biggest poker game in the whole territory, starting in two days' time,' the clerk informed them. His eyes travelled over every inch of the brothers' well-dressed figures.

Asa dipped the pen into the inkwell and started to write on the register.

'Of course we're here for the big game, Olin.' He kicked his brother's boot. 'That's why we've spent three days in that stagecoach.'

'Oh yeah.' Olin shrugged. 'I'm so tuckered after that stagecoach ride I can't even think straight. I sure can't wait for the big game to start.'

Asa Fenton looked at the clerk. 'My brother and I are expecting an old friend to call on us sometime in the next couple of days. When he calls can you send him up to our room?'

The clerk looked jealous. 'I guess so.' He sighed.

'Just business, you understand.' Olin blew a line of smoke at the floor.

The clerk smiled again. 'I understand.'

'What room are we in?' Asa asked.

The clerk reached behind him and pulled a key off the wall hooks. He handed it to Asa and returned the pen to its holder.

'Room seven.' He winked in a manner that made both the hired gunmen nervous. 'Lucky seven. If there's anything either of you gents want, just let me know. I'll surely oblige. Remember, anything.'

Asa cleared his throat. 'Ain't you the friendly one.'

'Friendlier than you could imagine.' The clerk winked.

'Thank you kindly,' Olin said through gritted teeth.

Both touched their hat brims and picked up their bags from the floor. They headed towards the wide-carpeted staircase and felt the clerk's eyes burning into their frock-coats as they mounted the steps.

'He'll oblige, Olin.'

'I figured as much, Asa.'

THREE

Hangman's Canyon was well named. The trees that filled the canyon, just south of War Smoke, had once been used to stretch the necks of many men before Matt Fallen had been appointed marshal. A score of its trees still bore rope scars on their sturdy branches. Due to its reputation few men ever chose to ride through the canyon, but Gentleman Joe Laker was no ordinary man.

The silver-haired gambler was daring, unlike most of his profession. Fear of being hanged was something to which he did not give a second thought. He stood in his stirrups and allowed his stallion to find its own pace through the array of trees.

News of the poker tournament had spread like

wildfire since the Longhorn saloon had announced it a few weeks earlier.

Dedicated gamblers like Gentleman Joe lived their entire lives hoping to win a pot such as the one the Longhorn was rumoured to be putting up.

Laker allowed his stallion to race down the canyon while he balanced like a cowboy in his stirrups. He knew that he was close to War Smoke. So close he could taste it. It was nearly five years since the gambler had last been to the sprawling settlement, but he had not forgotten the way.

His mount cleared the canyon and suddenly a range of tall grass stood before his snorting mount. Gentleman Joe reined in the stallion and allowed it to rest. While it chewed on the sweet grass the gambler gazed at the distant town.

Laker rested his wrists upon his saddle horn.

The gambler looked at the faint blur on the horizon. It looked insignificant from where he rested, but Gentleman Joe knew the truth. War Smoke was big. Bigger than most of the other towns in the territory, with more card tables even than Tombstone boasted.

He lifted his canteen and shook it.

The few mouthfuls of water remaining inside

the canteen were barely enough to wash the dust from his mouth but Laker knew that there was plenty of water in War Smoke.

He unscrewed the stopper and filled his mouth with the last of the precious liquid, then he returned the empty vessel to its resting place beside his coiled saddle rope. He pulled his leathers back on and lifted the head of his mount. He then tapped his spurs.

The stallion galloped on through the swaying grass towards the distant town. With each stride of his high-shouldered horse War Smoke drew closer and closer.

FOUR

Osceola was a small whitewashed adobe settlement to the east of War Smoke. It had fewer than twenty buildings and was as quiet as the grave. Its peaceful existence was about to be shattered as the sound of hoof beats rang out across the desert sand.

The inhabitants of the small village knew that a stranger was approaching, for the combined wealth of Osceola had never amounted to enough to buy even one horse.

The raven-haired people moved away from their homes and watched the approaching wall of dust as the deadly horseman emerged from its unholy depths.

Travis Grey had made good time since leaving

Red Rim on his journey to War Smoke. He glanced up at the sun in the cloudless heavens and pulled his hat brim to shade his eyes.

The horse cantered on as its master sat motionless upon its back. The people of Osceola had few visitors and the sight of anyone astride a horse was almost mesmerizing. To the innocent eyes watching him it was like looking at a god. The bright sun danced off the silver buckles adorning Grey's saddle. It was as if shafts of heavenly light were exploding from both the horse and rider.

None of the villagers had ever witnessed anything quite so spectacular before. They watched in awe as the stranger slowly came closer and closer.

Had they known what sort of man was approaching their tiny settlement they would have fled, but the sight of the rider teased their curiosity.

Grey allowed his mount to slow to a walk, then he stopped the animal with a swift jerk of his reins.

The people kept a respectful distance between him and themselves as they watched Travis Grey study the faces of the men, women and children.

It was impossible to tell who was most

impressed by the lethal killer. None of the people of the remote village had ever seen anyone like the sight the handsome Travis Grey presented to their eyes.

Grey slowly rose in his saddle and dismounted in one fluid action. He held his reins as he surveyed every single one of the people gathered around him.

'Any of you speak English?' Grey asked as his gloved hands tied his reins to a weathered tree trunk.

There was no response. The faces looked at the deadly killer blankly.

Travis Grey smiled. It was a cold-hearted smile. His eyes studied the people before him as he rested his thumbs on the grips of his guns.

'If you can't speak English then you can't go telling folks of what I'm about to do,' Grey observed.

His statement fell on deaf ears.

Not one word that left his mouth was understood by any of the people who encircled the venomous stranger. His wide grin should have alerted them to the danger he posed but they simply smiled back at him.

'I was all fired up getting to War Smoke and

killing me another lawman but I reckon I can afford to waste a little time here.' Grey laughed as he pulled out both of his guns and cocked their hammers.

The smiles on the faces of the villagers evaporated as quickly as the morning dew did once the blazing sun rose each day in this harsh climate.

Suddenly they realized that this was no god.

His smiling face was not that of someone who was amused but rather of someone who had evil intent infused into every devilish sinew.

The villagers suddenly backed away from Grey, but it was too late. With a deadly accuracy that could have only been learnt from Satan himself, Grey began shooting.

His targets were the men and older women. They arched and fell as his bullets ripped through them, but Grey was not finished killing.

He reloaded both his guns swiftly and started firing again. This time his targets were the cowering young men and children.

There was no mercy in either the demented Grey or his smoking weapons. He continued firing.

Travis Grey roared with laughter as bolts of lightning spewed from his gun barrels. This was a turkey-shoot and they were the turkeys.

The sand of Osceola was stained with blood and littered with the dead and wounded as Travis Grey shook the spent casings from his smoking guns again. His narrowed eyes watched what was left of the villagers as he pulled bullets from his belt and pushed them into the guns.

He holstered one gun and marched through the carnage to where two young females knelt in the pools of blood. He stared down at both the girls and laughed as they prayed to a deity who had been helpless to stop him.

Grey slid his other six-shooter into its holster and grabbed their manes of black hair. He twisted it around his wrists and marched towards one of the whitewashed adobes, dragging his screaming captives behind him.

They left a trail of deep grooves in the bloody sand as their naked heels vainly fought against Grey. The inside of the adobe was a lot cooler than the sun-bleached exterior but the deadly killer did not notice anything except the females he had saved for an equally gruesome fate.

He released his grip on them and was amused as they scrambled to the far wall. They were shocked and terrified as they huddled together and watched as the merciless gunman studied them. Grey looked from one to the other and tried to figure out which to choose first.

He strode towards them and salivated.

'Two juicy steaks dripping with gravy and I sure have me an appetite,' he drawled to the wide-eyed females. 'Killing always makes me hungry.'

Before either of the young females could defend herself, Grey had reached down and torn the bloodstained fabric from their tanned flesh. The more they fought the more excited he became. His hands ripped at their clothing until he had satisfied his depraved desire.

Lustfully he looked down upon them as they tried to cover themselves up with hands far too small to do so. Grey nodded and pointed at one of the girls.

Like whipped dogs they listened to his words. Neither of them understood what he was saying.

'It'll be a crying shame to kill you afterwards but that's the way it's gotta be,' he calmly informed them. 'That's just the way it's gotta be.'

FIVE

The Dixie was one of the smaller saloons in War Smoke, but even it had gaming tables and enough dance-hall girls to satisfy the needs of its varied patrons. It was said that it made more noise than any of its larger competitors, but as the two drifters sat at a table at the foot of a rickety staircase the Dixie was unusually quiet.

Sam Poole and Frank Akins stared at the thimble glasses before them and the half-consumed bottle of whiskey they shared. Poole glanced around the saloon and beat on the table with his fingers.

Akins grunted. 'Quit fretting, Sam.'

Poole leaned forward, filled his glass with whiskey and stared at his companion.

45

'I reckon we bit off way too much this time, Frank,' he said. 'I'm for ducking out of this deal before we get ourselves in deep trouble.'

Akins was a pug-nosed man. His wrinkled features did not seem to match his dark hair. He might have been older than his cohort but it was hard to tell. The dust that still covered the seated couple hid many clues to what they actually looked like.

'It'll be an easy two hundred dollars, Sam,' Akins said as he poured another whiskey. 'The easiest money we've earned in months. You can run if you like, but I'm keeping the money if you do.'

Poole exhaled and picked his teeth with his thumbnail.

'I still ain't so sure about this job, Frank,' he confided. 'I'm no hired gun.'

'I am.' Akins nodded.

Poole quickly downed his whiskey and poured himself another glass.

'Stealing horses and rustling a few head of cattle is one thing but this is a lot more serious, Frank,' he pointed out. 'I'm just feared that this might be a trick. That *hombre* could be just setting us up.'

'He wouldn't dare, Sam,' Akins growled. 'We made a bargain and it works both ways.'

'We ain't even set eyes on the dude that hired us, Frank,' Poole fretted. 'Two halves of one-hundred-dollar bills in a damn letter brung us here. How'd we know he'll even pay up if we do his killing for him?'

Frank Akins tapped his hideous nose. 'He didn't sign that letter he sent us but I know who he is. I figured it out.'

'How'd you do that?'

Akins roared with laughter. 'We only know one critter in War Smoke, Sam. Think about it. It has to be him that wrote that letter and sent us the torn-up money, don't it?'

Sam Poole blinked hard and tried to clear his whiskey-fumed mind. Then he nodded.

'Why'd we come here anyway, Frank?' he wondered. 'That fat old dude would be out by two hundred bucks and we'd be free and clear.'

'That fat old dude sent us the short halves of them bills, idiot.' Akins rested an elbow on the tabletop and pointed a finger at his trail pal. 'They ain't worth a plug nickel without the other halves with the numbers on them.'

'They ain't?'

Akins exhaled. 'You agreed to this just like I done, Sam. You can't go turning yella now.'

For a moment Poole frowned; then he leaned close to Akins once more. His eyes were bulging as his thoughts drifted to the lawman they had seen on their arrival in War Smoke.

'Did you see the size of that marshal when we rode into town, Frank?' Poole shuddered when he spoke. 'That critter is as big as a tree. I don't cotton to going up against him. He looks darn mean.'

'We won't tangle with Matt Fallen, Sam.' Akins downed his whiskey. 'We just do our killing and then we ride out. By the time Fallen figures out what's happened we'll be out of the territory.'

'What if that lawman stops us?'

Akins shook his head. 'Why would he? That big poker game will probably keep Fallen so busy he won't know if he's coming or going.'

'You reckon?'

'I sure do.' Akins smiled. 'Marshal Fallen probably won't even have himself time to get any shuteye until that poker tournament is on.'

'How long do them games tend to last, Frank?'

'I heard stories that some of them poker games can last weeks or even longer, Sam.' Akins chuckled. 'Matt Fallen will be a dribbling zombie by the time we earn our money. They'll need toothpicks to keep his eyes open.'

Sam Poole rubbed the dust-covered sweat from his mouth and looked around the saloon. He learned over the damp table.

'What if he's seen your picture on a poster, Frank?' Poole whispered. 'If he recognizes you he'll be trying to lay claim to your bounty.'

Frank Akins laughed even louder.

'A lot of star-packers have tried but none of them has even come close.' The drifter spat. 'Besides, there ain't no photograph of me on any Wanted posters, Sam. All they got is a sketch. A stinking sketch. Fallen will never put two and two together.'

Sam Poole sighed heavily and stared at the floor.

'I sure hope you're right, Frank,' he muttered.

Akins grunted, lifted the whiskey bottle and held it over the thimble glasses. His icy glare looked determined as they bored into his cohort.

'I'm always right, Sam,' he declared confidently. He refilled their glasses with yet more of the amber liquor. 'Now drink up and quit fretting.'

Poole lifted his glass and threw the whiskey into

his mouth. As it burned its way down into his guts a smile crept across his face.

'Let's go pay that fat old dude a visit, Frank,' he suggested.

Akins patted his pal's shoulder. 'Now you're talking my kind of lingo, pard.'

SIX

Both Fallen and Elmer came round the corner into Front Street and gave sighs of relief. Both lawmen had covered the majority of streets on their rounds and were grateful that their journey was over at least until later. The afternoon sun was a lot cooler than when they had set out but Matt Fallen was dry and almost thirsty enough to consider drinking some of Elmer's strange beverages.

The marshal looked at his deputy and the holstered gun strapped to his lean frame. No matter how many times he scolded Elmer the young man never seemed to like wearing the weapon.

'I guess I'd best get over to the office and start rustling up that coffee for you, Marshal Fallen,'

Elmer said as he kept adjusting the hefty gun and holster. 'I bet you're mighty thirsty.'

Fallen eyed his deputy and sat down on the edge of a trough. He did not answer as his eyes studied the busy street and the two distant horses left outside the Dixie earlier by the drifters.

'How long do you reckon we've been away from here, Elmer?'

Elmer shrugged. 'Best part of an hour, I guess. Why, Marshal Fallen?'

Fallen pointed to the distant horses. 'That black roan with the white stockings is still hitched up outside the Dixie.'

The deputy scratched his head and held his holster in the way folks hold up their pants when unsure how secure they are.

'How come you're so darn interested in that black roan, Marshal Fallen?' he asked. 'When you seen one horse you seen them all.'

Fallen shook his head. 'Black roans are rare, Elmer. Every one of them is different and they're all mighty expensive. How do you reckon a drifter could afford himself a horse of that quality?'

'Maybe he stole it.'

Fallen grinned. 'Now you're thinking like a lawman.'

'What time is it, Marshal Fallen?' Elmer asked. He rested his shoulder against a porch upright and stared along the still-busy thoroughfare. 'I'm plumb tuckered carrying this heavy gun around.'

Fallen stood and removed his hat for long enough to shake the accumulated sweat from it.

'You know I never carry me a timepiece, Elmer.' He sighed and then added, 'Maybe if I did I might know how late you always are.'

Elmer inhaled deeply and stared across the street at the café. The aroma of cooking made the deputy swallow hard.

'I'm kinda hungry,' Elmer said, rubbing his slim belly. 'Can't we have us some grub?'

'Don't tell me,' Fallen grumbled. 'You're broke again.'

Elmer raised his eyebrows. 'How'd you know that?'

'You're always broke.'

'There's just too many darn days in the month, Marshal Fallen,' Elmer told him with a sigh. 'Ain't my fault my wages don't stretch.'

Matt Fallen smiled. 'When you're dead I'll have to keep paying you for two months before we break even, Elmer.'

'I am powerful hungry.' Elmer glanced at the marshal with sorrowful eyes.

Fallen grinned. 'OK. I'll buy you dinner.'

Both men stepped down from the boardwalk and crossed to the café on the corner. As they were about to enter Fallen stopped again and stared down to where the two drifters' mounts were still tethered.

Elmer held on to the doorknob and waited.

'That's just them drifters' horses, Marshal Fallen,' he said as the aroma of freshly cooked food filled his nostrils.

Fallen did not respond to his words. He just continued to stare at the horses curiously. He thought about the words of warning the stage-coach driver had spoken to him earlier.

'Marshal Fallen?' Elmer said, loud enough to draw the lawman's attention. 'I'm real powerful hungry.'

Fallen rubbed his thumb along his jaw, then turned and trailed his deputy into the café. He had no sooner removed his hat than he heard the distinctive tones of the town's only medical man.

'Now what's caught your interest, Matt?' Doc Weaver asked as he chewed on his pipe-stem.

'Nothing, Doc,' Fallen replied. He pulled out a chair and seated himself opposite his oldest friend in War Smoke. 'I was just looking at a couple of drifters' horses.'

'You need yourself a good woman, Matt,' Doc said.

'Is that your professional opinion, Doc?' Fallen asked.

'When you find one try and find out if she's got a sister,' answered Doc, and he chuckled.

Elmer dragged out a chair and sat down between the two old friends. He tucked a napkin into his collar and grabbed a knife and fork in readiness.

'I'm having me a steak, Doc,' he informed Weaver.

'I'm mighty pleased for you, Elmer.' Doc Weaver had already reached his dessert and was toying with what remained of his apple pie. He removed the pipe from his lips and pointed it at the marshal. 'You look kinda jittery, Matt.'

Fallen smiled. 'I thought I recognized one of them drifters, Doc.'

Doc Weaver grinned.

'War Smoke is crawling with drifters, Matt,' he said in a fatherly tone. 'You can't fret on all of them. Relax for long enough to eat a meal. That's advice from your doctor.'

'I reckon you're right, Doc,' Fallen said, but his thoughts kept drifting to the words spoken to him by the stagecoach crew.

Elmer grinned like a Cheshire cat.

'Marshal Fallen is buying me dinner, Doc,' he ventured. 'I'm having me a steak with gravy and onions.'

Doc raised his bushy eyebrows and looked at Fallen. 'You'll regret fattening young Elmer up, Matt. Mark my words, there ain't nothing worse than a fat deputy.'

Fallen smiled. He leaned on his elbows and watched the well-endowed waitress approaching. Her entire upper half seemed to wobble with every step.

'Howdy, Matt,' she purred like a well-proportioned cat. 'What can I get you?'

'Two steaks, Maisie,' he told her. 'I'm treating Elmer.'

'You spoil that boy.' She smiled and then filled their cups with the blackest coffee in War Smoke. 'It'll be about ten minutes, Marshal.'

'Thank you kindly.' Fallen nodded.

Doc turned and looked at Elmer. 'Tell me,

Elmer. Are you still strutting out with that red-haired gal that works in the Longhorn?'

'I surely am.' Elmer grinned.

Doc looked across the table at the marshal and winked.

'I gotta admit it, Matt. Elmer sure has an eye for women.'

'That he does, Doc.'

'Considering that gal ain't got a tooth in her head,' Doc added wryly. 'Elmer is still sniffing around her like a faithful hound.'

Elmer frowned. 'Hold on there, Doc. Miss Clara has got teeth. A whole bunch of them.'

'Really?' Doc smiled and patted the deputy on the arm. 'If that's what she's telling you then who am I to disagree?'

'Tell Doc to quit telling lies, Marshal Fallen.'

'Doc don't mean no harm, Elmer.' Fallen smiled, lifted his cup to his lips and sipped at the coffee. 'He's just joshing.'

The deputy leaned towards the sawbones.

'Marshal Fallen said them drifters was ghosts, Doc,' he said, giggling. 'Mind you, they was covered in a whole heap of trail dust. They did kinda look like ghosts.'

Doc nodded. 'Matt might be right, Elmer.'

Elmer looked blankly at Doc. 'What you mean, Doc? Everyone knows there ain't no such thing as ghosts.'

Doc struck a match and sucked its flame into his pipe bowl. He rose to his feet and stared down at the young lawman. He tossed a silver dollar next to his plate.

'So you don't believe in ghosts, Elmer?' he asked.

'I surely don't, Doc,' Elmer stammered. 'Everybody knows there ain't no such animal as a ghost.'

Fuelled by mischief, Doc leaned over Elmer and whispered into the deputy's ear.

'But do they believe in you, boy?' he asked. He turned to go out into the afternoon sun. 'Ask yourself. Do they believe in you?'

The young deputy sat with a confused expression upon his face as he tried to understand the question.

Matt Fallen placed his cup on the table and nudged his deputy. Elmer nearly jumped out of his skin as he was abruptly brought back to reality.

'What?' he croaked nervously. 'You done scared me half to death, Marshal Fallen. You oughta be careful. I'm armed.'

'Our steaks are coming, Elmer.' The marshal grinned as he pointed to Maisie, carrying two large white plates towards them.

The inch-thick steaks filled the sizeable plates which the waitress set before the two lawmen. They sizzled beneath a blanket of onions and fried potatoes. Fallen started to cut his way into the welcome meal as his confused deputy simply looked at his own plate.

'Eat up, Elmer,' the marshal said encouragingly.

A troubled Elmer looked at Fallen.

'What do you reckon Doc meant, Marshal Fallen?' he asked the man he respected more than any other.

'He was just teasing you, Elmer,' Fallen answered, chewing on his steak. 'You know old Doc. He just likes to ruffle feathers.'

The expression on Elmer's face still looked confused as he half-heartedly cut into his own aromatic dinner.

'How can ghosts believe in us if they don't exist?' he wondered. 'That just don't make no sense. It don't make no sense at all. Or does it, Marshal Fallen?'

'It's just a riddle,' Fallen told him.

'But it don't make no sense.'

As Fallen chewed he turned around and looked out through the front windows of the café. The drifters' horses were still tied to the hitching rail outside the busy saloon halfway along Front Street. Fallen focused on the black roan with two white stockings, which was still hitched up outside the Longhorn. The marshal turned back to face his deputy.

'You're right, Elmer,' he drawled, trying to dismiss everything from his thoughts apart from his flavoursome meal. 'It don't make any sense at all.'

Elmer grinned and started to eat. 'You know something, Marshal Fallen?'

'What?'

The deputy raised an eyebrow. 'I don't give a hoot if ghosts don't believe in me.'

As the marshal carved himself another chunk off the massive steak the entire café rocked. The deafening sound of a double-barrelled shotgun being fired filled the small eatery.

Fallen dropped his cutlery and wiped his mouth with a napkin. He rose to his feet and dashed to the door. He turned the brass door-knob and stepped out on to the porch.

The ear-splitting noise still echoed all around Front Street. Fallen wondered where the hefty weapon had been discharged but there was no need to ask anyone. A crowd of people had stopped in their tracks and were pointing at a side street which led to the poorer section of War Smoke.

'It came from over there, Marshal,' one man ventured.

'Somewhere down in the alleyways by the sound of it, Matt,' another added.

Matt Fallen ran to where everyone was either looking or pointing. By the time he had reached the side street he had drawn his trusty Peacemaker.

At the end of the crowded side street he ran into a narrow fenced alley. He kept running down the alley. With each step the shadows grew denser and darker. The houses that backed on to the alley had been built hastily. They were touching like stacked decks of cards, with hardly any distance between any of them. As Fallen raced through the alley he noticed that although the sky was still blue, very little of the sun's warming light ever reached this section of War Smoke.

He rounded a tight corner and skidded to a stop.

The eerie light ahead of him was almost like the dead of night, he thought. He walked slowly with his gun in his outstretched hand.

Fallen could hear stabled horses to his left and realized that he must be directly behind the stage-coach livery. He rubbed his nose in a vain attempt to rid it of the conflicting smells which grew stronger the deeper he travelled into the shadows.

The scent of horses mingled with the stench of poverty, but as he strode forward another more telling aroma filled his nostrils.

It was the smell of gunsmoke.

His eyes narrowed as they searched the dark-ness. He could see the bluish haze floating on the air.

This was where the shotgun had unleashed its fury, he told himself. He was getting close to where the shotgun had expelled its cartridges.

As the marshal carefully approached another bend in the high fences another grim notion occurred to Fallen. What if the double-barrelled weapon had only been fired to lure him here?

What if there was someone waiting to see the

tin star he proudly wore upon his vest front? Fallen had been the target of many a gunman's barrel over the years.

Then he reached the corner. He paused as he looked around into the darkest part of the narrow back alleyway. For a moment the marshal did not know what he was looking upon. The lane was littered with garbage and discarded goods.

Fallen took a deep breath and decided that there was only one way he was ever going to find out what lay ahead, and that was to keep moving.

He had taken barely three more steps before his eyes understood.

The marshal paused and glared down upon the crumpled carcass that filled the width of the alley. Fallen had a stomach which was stronger than most but even he had never seen anything as brutal as this before.

Whoever lay dead before him was unrecognizable.

Both barrels of a scattergun had been fired at the dead man's head at almost point-blank range. Whoever this was he had not stood a chance, the marshal thought. Fallen knelt down beside the victim and tried to tell who it was that he was looking upon. No matter how hard he tried there was no face or head left upon the bloodstained shoulders.

The lawman glanced at the wooden fence behind the body. It was peppered with buckshot and splashed with gore. Even the shadows could not hide the obvious brutality that had ended the life of this man.

Then as Fallen moved the body he noticed the golden chain covered in gore. He pulled the chain and a half-hunter watch appeared from a vest pocket.

The marshal grabbed the round, golden time-piece, flicked the lid open and stared at the dedication engraved inside.

For Joel Erikson on your retirement. Fallen read the inscription. Then he dropped the watch and stood up. He wiped the blood from his fingers down his pants and shook his head.

Erikson had worked for the brewery situated at the far end of War Smoke for over ten years. The old man had retired only two months earlier. It did not seem a fitting end for one who had given so much pleasure to so many thirsty men.

Fallen continued to look down upon what was left of the old man and rubbed his hand over his face.

'Why would anyone kill you, Joel?' Fallen asked the corpse as he tried to find a reason for the slaying.

Then he heard the sound of movement behind him.

Fallen cocked his six-shooter and waited as the noise grew louder in the narrow alleyway. He gritted his teeth and kept the gun aimed at the corner.

'Are you down here, Marshal Fallen?' Elmer's voice rang out as he stumbled around the corner. The deputy stopped even more abruptly than the marshal had done.

Fallen released the hammer and slid his Peacemaker into its holster. He rested his knuckles on his hips and looked down again at the lifeless remnant of what had until only minutes earlier been a retired brewer.

'Who is that?' Elmer asked as cautiously he approached his boss and the gruesome sight by the marshal's boots.

'This used to be Joel Erikson,' Fallen replied. He looked around the dark shadows for any sign of the killer. 'He used to work over yonder at the brewery.'

Elmer grimaced at what was left of the brewer.

'Lord above, this is a crying shame, Marshal Fallen. Darn pitiful.'

'Yep,' the marshal agreed.

'Shall I go tell the undertaker?' Elmer asked.

Fallen shook his head.

'Nope, we don't need the undertaker. I reckon its best we carry what's left of this fine old man out of here, Elmer,' he said. 'It's the least we can do for old Joel.'

Elmer nodded. 'Kinda respectful like.'

Matt Fallen positioned himself just behind the mutilated head and shoulders of the blood-soaked corpse. He then glanced at his deputy and queried:

'Tell me something. What took you so damn long catching up with me, Elmer?'

'I was eating the dinner you bought me, Marshal Fallen,' Elmer replied honestly. 'You know that.'

The marshal bent down and grabbed hold of the torso while Elmer took the legs. They both straightened up and held what was left of Joel Erikson between them.

'That steak took an awful lot of chewing, Marshal Fallen,' Elmer added. 'I ate it as quickly as I could and then come looking for you. Maisie told me to tell you that she done put your meal in the oven to keep it warm.'

Matt Fallen nodded as they carefully carried their hefty burden along the alley. Blood dripped between the marshal's fingers.

'I've kinda lost my appetite, Elmer,' he said.

SEVEN

The gambler had not used his spurs for the previous few miles over which his stallion had galloped across the swaying grass towards the outskirts of War Smoke. There was no need to urge the horse on, for its own thirst was doing that. The scent of precious water filled the animal's snorting nostrils as it forged its way onwards.

All the famed gambler known as Gentleman Joe Laker had to do was stand in his stirrups and allow the powerful stallion to race towards the nearest water trough.

War Smoke had an abundance of many things it did not require but it also had a plentiful supply of crystal-clear water.

Dust kicked up from the stallion's hoofs rose up

into the sky as the rays of the setting sun turned the clouds the colour of blood. The day was dying just like the pitiful innocents in the town below. The lone horseman was eager to reach War Smoke before the darkness of night hampered his progress.

Laker felt as though his entire existence had been leading up to this very moment. The news of the poker game seemed to be meant for him alone. For years the silver-haired gambler had managed to make a bare living from his skill and judgement with playing cards, but he had never yet been able to win the truly big game.

The one life-changing game that would make his reputation had so far eluded him.

Gentleman Joe had heard of others who had become wealthy overnight as they had managed to beat the odds and collect all of the poker chips but so far he had not been able to join their ranks.

When he had read of the big poker tournament to be held at the Longhorn saloon Gentleman Joe Laker felt that his luck was at last about to change for the better. In his mind it seemed to him as though everything had been leading to this moment in his life.

Most gamblers wait a lifetime for that one

moment when the omens are in their favour. For Laker reading the newspaper story was as if fate was tapping him on the shoulder and pointing the way to go.

He drove his mount on towards War Smoke.

He arrived well ahead of the start of the big game and knew that everything was looking favourable. The gambler sat down on his saddle and caught his breath.

Gentleman Joe Laker had not wanted to arrive late for the big poker game in War Smoke. He had been drawn away from his usual haunts to War Smoke like a hundred other men who also dreamt of winning their own personal fortune. Laker, however, had acquired more than his renowned skill as a poker player in the years he had plied his trade. He had also learned how to use his guns. It was a necessity when you played as well as he did.

His hands were not only capable of making cards appear and disappear at will, they also had the speed to draw and fire his secreted weaponry faster than most men could blink their eyes.

This would be his last chance at proving to himself that he could be the best poker player in the Wild West. The tournament would be his final opportunity to prove that Gentleman Joe Laker was indeed the best card player alive.

A mixture of greed, hope and self-belief came over Laker as he rode through the sprawling town and slowly its myriad lanterns were lighted. Towns like War Smoke did not let the coming of darkness hamper their activities. The illumination provided by the coal-tar lanterns allowed the players to continue playing through the night as well.

War Smoke seemed like a sea of fireflies to the intrepid horseman. The entire town was glowing in amber light as Laker entered its outskirts.

As the heavens darkened to crimson the determined rider slowed his pace. The trail led down through what was commonly known as Boot Hill.

Laker eyed the scores of wooden markers dotted across the rolling hills. It was an ominous warning of his likely fate should he not be aware of the dangers he was about to face.

A good poker player was seldom greeted with thanks when he dragged his opponent's poker chips towards him. Some folks accepted defeat gracefully but a few considered that anyone who bested them at cards had to be dealing from the bottom of the deck.

Whenever a certain breed of poker player lost their stake to Laker he knew they would start shouting 'Cheat' and follow the insult with hot lead. Gentleman Joe glanced down at the hundred or more wooden markers as his high-stepping stallion walked between them.

No wonder there were so many markers on Boot Hill, he thought. War Smoke had more gambling halls and saloons than any other town in the territory.

A lot of gamblers were buried on that hill. Some had been bad and some had been good. They had all been slow on the draw.

He narrowed his eyes and focused upon the dust of another traveller coming across the vast cattle range from the east.

The rider was moving far more quickly than his observer.

'Somebody's sure in a hurry,' Laker muttered under his breath. He steered his mount down the dry hillside until they reached level ground.

Gentleman Joe Laker allowed the stallion to resume its pace towards the welcoming water troughs that were dotted all along the main thoroughfare. The scent of fresh-pumped water in the numerous troughs throughout War Smoke was making the stallion eager to reach them.

The seasoned gambler was not troubled by the sight of another rider. He knew that War Smoke would probably be full to bursting with men of his profession before the poker game began.

The setting sun was now only just above the horizon. He knew that it would disappear before either he or the unknown rider could enter War Smoke.

He rested a hand on one of his holstered guns and eyed the town carefully as his thirsty horse gathered pace. It was a pointless exercise because he knew that the true danger for men of his profession was never to be found when they were approaching a town.

The real danger was when they were inside its boundaries or attempting to leave with their winnings.

Laker glanced at the heavens. The sky was now a violent mixture of red and black stripes. Slowly stars emerged from their hiding-places and twinkled as the stallion cantered through the outskirts of War Smoke.

He allowed the horse to stop at the first trough in Front Street. As the stallion filled its belly the gambler sat watching the busy streets.

He had forgotten how big War Smoke was. The sight of so many people also took him by surprise as he sat astride the drinking horse.

Gentleman Joe Laker took a long slim cigar, gripped it between his teeth and lit it with a match. He inhaled deeply and watched as the other rider steered his horse into the long street at the far end of town. For a moment he was unable to make out who the rider was but as he came nearer Gentleman Joe Laker felt his heart quicken. The amber light of scores of coal-tar lanterns was sufficient to reveal the familiar features to Laker's knowing eyes.

The gambler pulled the cigar from his mouth and allowed the line of smoke to filter from between his teeth. He nodded to himself.

He had encountered the youthful rider several times before on his many journeys across the vast country and knew exactly what the innocent-looking horseman was capable of. He had seen how the merciless killer would simply end the life of whoever he chose to destroy.

'Travis Grey.' Laker said the name as though he were chewing on poison. 'Whatever that varmint is doing here in War Smoke it ain't got nothing to do with poker.'

His heart was pounding inside his chest as he watched Grey guide his horse into the livery stable. Gentleman Joe gathered up his reins and tapped his spurs against the flanks of his own mount.

The gambler knew there was another livery stable at the opposite end of the settlement, well away from where Travis Grey was leaving his horse.

Laker negotiated the crowded street and put as much distance between himself and the heartless creature as possible. As his stallion reached the other livery set just off the main street he saw the familiar figure of Matt Fallen emerge from the funeral parlour with his deputy at his shoulder.

Matt Fallen was a welcome sight compared to Travis Grey.

Gentleman Joe stopped his mount outside the large open doors of the livery stable. He dismounted and then saw Fallen walking towards him.

Laker was about to greet the lawmen when he saw that they were covered in blood. For a moment he assumed the crimson gore belonged to the marshal and his deputy, but as they drew closer he could see that neither of the lawmen appeared injured.

'Are you boys OK?' Laker asked. 'You look like you've bin wrestling with a freshly slaughtered steer.'

Fallen stopped and eyed up the silver-haired gambler.

'Well, if it ain't Gentleman Joe Laker,' he greeted the gambler.

Laker ducked under the neck of his horse. 'I'm serious, Matt. How in tarnation did you get so messed up?'

Fallen sighed and mopped his brow on his sleeve.

'Somebody got themselves murdered a while back, Joe,' Fallen informed the gambler. 'Me and Elmer carried what was left of him to the funeral parlour.'

Elmer edged forward. 'It was Joel Erikson. Got his head blown clean off his shoulders. Me and Marshal Fallen reckon the killer used a scatter-gun.'

Fallen looked more closely at the gambler. 'You just arrived in town, Joe?'

Laker nodded. 'A few minutes back,' he said. 'I ain't the only critter to arrive here, Matt. I just seen Travis Grey steer his nag into the stable down

Front Street.'

Fallen raised an eyebrow.

'Travis Grey?' He repeated the name and rubbed his jaw. 'Are you sure?'

'Dead sure, Matt,' Gentleman Joe Laker assured Fallen. 'Grey ain't the kind of varmint you forget in a hurry.'

Elmer looked puzzled. 'Who in tarnation is Travis Grey, Marshal Fallen? I ain't ever heard about him.'

The tall lawman glanced at his deputy.

'He's trouble, Elmer. Real big trouble.'

'A merciless killer.' Laker patted his arm.

'Then let's go find that critter and arrest him, Marshal Fallen,' Elmer innocently suggested. 'We already got one killer roaming War Smoke. We sure don't want another one.'

'It ain't that easy, Elmer,' Fallen said with a snort. 'Travis Grey is a maniac but nobody has ever bin able to prove it in the eyes of the law. He kills folks for no better reason than he likes killing.'

'He ain't wanted?' Elmer gasped.

Both Fallen and Laker shook their heads.

'Then what are we gonna do?' the deputy wondered.

Fallen shrugged. 'I'm gonna go back to the jail and find me a clean shirt. I suggest you head on over to your ma and do the same, Elmer.'

'I meant, what are we gonna do about Travis Grey, Marshal Fallen?' Elmer sighed.

'We ain't gonna do nothing,' Fallen said firmly. 'We can't touch Grey until he breaks the law. Savvy? We gotta catch him breaking the law.'

'I sure wish you luck, Matt,' Gentleman Joe said. He turned and led his horse into the livery, where he was greeted by the stableman.

Elmer moved closer to the marshal and whispered.

'Are you serious? We can't do nothing until we catch that madman in the act?' he questioned.

Matt Fallen placed a large hand on his deputy's shoulder and guided him back to Front Street. He paused on the corner near the Diamond Pin Hotel.

'Go home and change that shirt, Elmer,' he said. 'I'll head on back to the office and find me one that ain't covered in old Joel's blood.'

Elmer smiled from ear to ear.

'Then I can make that coffee you bin looking forward to trying.' He winked.

Matt Fallen rested his hand on his gun grip and

set off through the lantern light towards the jail. The street was even busier than it had been before the sun had set.

EIGHT

Doyle Sanders sat in his office at the rear of the Longhorn saloon and knew that in just over a day the big poker tournament would start. He had already noticed that there were more than a hundred new faces in War Smoke and all of them belonged to famed gamblers. He had drawn the best poker players from across the territory to his saloon with the promise of the largest pot in history.

Not even the worst gambler seemed able to resist the temptation of winning the largest sum of money any of them had ever heard of being offered as the prize money.

As Sanders sat behind his oak desk and contemplated the forthcoming increase in his profits he heard someone tapping on his office door.

The rotund Sanders looked up from his ledger, picked his cigar out of the glass ashtray and returned it to his mouth. He struck a match and lit the cigar. He inhaled deeply and savoured its strong flavour.

'Come in,' he called through a cloud of smoke.

The door opened and Sanders beheld the familiar face of Bob King staring at him through the hazy mist that Sanders's cigar had created while he was doing his accounts.

'Can I have a word, Doyle?' King asked.

'The owner of the Lucky Dollar saloon can always come and see me,' Sanders replied. His plump fingers tapped the ash from his cigar into the tray. He gestured to a vacant chair. 'Come in and sit yourself down.'

'Thanks.' King closed the door and moved across the room towards his competitor. He sat down, looking unusually nervous.

'What can I do for you, Bob?' Sanders asked. He poured brandy into two elegantly crafted glasses. 'This is a business matter, I imagine?'

King loosened his collar. His gaze darted around the room and its walls lined with books.

'It's not exactly a business matter,' he said, 'but

it might be. I ain't too sure. That's why I'm here to talk it over with you.'

'Talk what over?' Sanders looked curious.

Bob King leaned forward and whispered, 'It's kinda delicate, Doyle. I ain't sure where to start.'

Sanders puffed on his cigar. 'I've always found the best place to start is the beginning, Bob. Maybe you should try that.'

King cleared his throat. 'There are a number of rumours going around town,' he said.

'Rumours?' Sanders watched King pick up one of the glasses of brandy before he lifted his own and inhaled its fragrance. 'What kind of rumours are we talking about?'

King took a big swallow and looked right across the desk at the man who seemed to have a knack of turning everything he touched into money. He loosened his collar.

'They reckon there are hired killers in War Smoke and you hired them, Doyle,' he told Sanders, his words coming out in a rush.

Doyle Sanders raised both his bushy eyebrows.

'Who the hell told you that, Bob?'

'Ain't it true?' King queried.

'I sure didn't.' Sanders took a mouthful of brandy and swallowed. He returned his cigar to the corner of his mouth. 'Why on earth would I do something like that?'

King shrugged his shoulders. 'I don't know. I figured that you would have a damn good reason, though.'

Sanders shook his head. 'Where did you hear such rumours?' the affluent saloon owner asked. 'Who on earth would be spreading such nonsense around?'

King finished his liquor and placed the empty glass on the desk. He loosened his collar again and looked around the lamp lit office.

'The rumours are rife, Doyle,' he said. 'There are more stories flying around town than flies in an outhouse.'

Sanders gripped the cigar in his teeth and rose. He followed his large belly around the office, leaving a trail of smoke over his shoulder.

'I think that maybe you should tell me a few of these stories, Bob,' he said. 'No matter how out-rageous they are, I want to know what is being said about me.'

King reached for the decanter and refilled his glass.

'You ain't gonna like what's being said about you, Doyle. You might even get mad,' King said.

He took a gulp of brandy to calm his nerves. 'I don't want you getting mad at me just 'coz I'm telling you these things.'

Sanders paused and looked at his fellow saloon owner. He forced a smile in hopes of learning the truth.

'Tell me everything you've heard, Bob,' he said calmly. 'I promise you that I shall not get angry with you.'

There was a long pause, then King started to relate the rumours he had overheard.

'Somebody reckons that you only staged the poker game to fill the streets of War Smoke with so many folks that nobody would notice your hired killers,' King gasped. 'I also heard tell that you want Marshal Fallen killed.'

Sanders puffed on his cigar thoughtfully. 'Continue.'

'I heard a rumour only this morning about you hiring two killers to kill Mort Heely the banker,' King went on. 'There are two drifters over in the Dixie right now and folks reckon they're your hired gunmen, Doyle.'

Sanders scratched his clean-shaven chin. 'Seems as though there's a lot of gossip in town. I appear to want a lot of folks dead, but none of this is true. Why would I hire killers?'

Bob King stood and downed the last of his brandy. His shaking hand placed the glass next to the decanter and he shuffled towards Sanders.

'Sorry if I upset you, Doyle,' he said. 'But I reckoned that it was best somebody tell you. I'd hate for something else to happen and you getting the blame.'

Sanders gripped King's sleeve. 'What do you mean by "something else" happening, Bob?' he asked. 'What has happened already?'

Bob King looked straight at Sanders.

'Somebody got their head blown off, Doyle,' he said. 'The marshal and his deputy carried the body to the funeral parlour not ten minutes ago.'

'Who got his head shot off?'

King shrugged. 'I don't know, Doyle. They reckoned the body was unrecognizable.'

Sanders pulled the cigar from his mouth and spat smoke at the floor as his mind raced. 'Do you reckon that my staging the poker tournament might have something to do with these rumours and the killing, Bob?'

'Damned if I know, Doyle,' King replied. 'But I'd be careful if I was you. Something's going on in town and I got me a real bad feeling about it.'

Doyle Sanders said nothing as he watched King leave his office. The large man moved back to his desk and stared at his safe in the corner. It held the vast sum of money he had advertised as the first prize of the poker tournament. He felt uneasy for the very first time in his life.

It was unsightly for a fat man to sweat, he told himself as he poured himself another large brandy. He held the crystal glass in the palm of his hand and swirled the amber liquor until it resembled a whirlpool.

Sweat ran down his temple and rolled over his double chin. He swallowed the contents of the tumbler and waited for the fumes to clear his head.

For a few moments he considered King's words; then he knew exactly what he had to do. He had to find the marshal and relate his fears to the only man in War Smoke who did not have a dishonest bone in his body.

I've got to talk to Matt Fallen Sanders told himself. He placed the crystal tumbler down on his ink blotter. *With all the money I've got in that damn safe I might have just made myself a target.*

The grim notion burned in his mind for what felt like an eternity. He blew down the funnel of his lamp and extinguished its flame.

Sanders marched across the office, grabbed his hat off the stand and opened the door. He stepped through the doorway, then thrust a key into the keyhole. He locked the door and placed the key into his vest pocket.

Doyle Sanders did not go into the cavernous saloon room which was crowded with regular patrons as well as nearly all the strangers he had lured into War Smoke. He instead made his way out of the Longhorn by way of one of its side doors.

The alley beside the Longhorn was dark in comparison with the interior of the brightly illuminated saloon but Sanders did not mind the shadows. They concealed the troubled expression which was drawn over his face.

Doyle Sanders had somewhere to go and someone to see. He knew that if anyone could advise him as to what he ought to do to protect himself and his prize money it was Matt Fallen.

He watched the crowds passing in the street as he made his way towards it at a pace which was not fitting for either his station in life or his weight.

Sanders strode down the alley until he reached the front of his saloon. He made his way to the busy street and was about to cross its wide expanse when something caught his attention. He squinted through the gloom towards a streetlight at the end of the saloon's boardwalk.

The large man moved to the side of a string of horses and peered over their saddles. Two men were standing and talking below the streetlight.

The oil lantern's glow revealed the features of both men.

Sanders knew one of them.

It was Bob King.

No matter how hard he tried Sanders could not recognize the other man. He was totally unknown to him. Sanders focused on the hand-tooled gun-belt strapped around the stranger's hips and felt his throat tighten.

Even saloon owners who rode nothing more dangerous than their oak desks knew that there was only one kind of man who sported such gun-belts.

Gunmen.

Hired gunmen were unlike most other folks, he told his pounding heart. They made sure that their holsters and belts were perfectly crafted so that they could draw their six-shooters with unri-valled speed.

Doyle Sanders rubbed his sweat-soaked face as he vainly attempted to overhear their conversation. Normally he would not have been troubled by the sight but there was something nagging at him.

Then he realized what it was which troubled him.

Bob King was smiling from ear to ear. It was like watching someone who had just told the funniest joke anyone had ever heard. Sanders had a feeling that the joke had been played on him.

Sanders frowned. He wondered why his fellow saloon owner had looked so grim back in his office and now, only minutes later, seemed a different person.

King pulled out his wallet and dealt banknotes as if they were playing cards to the stranger. The unknown man nodded and pushed the greenbacks into his coat pocket.

Bob King had paid money to the stranger.

Why? The question haunted the troubled owner of the Longhorn saloon. Sanders had rarely seen Bob King smile in all the time he had been in War Smoke. Yet now he was grinning from all over his face and that frightened Sanders.

The large man waited while both men walked

the short distance to the Lucky Dollar and disappeared inside before he ventured away from the horses.

Sanders hastily crossed the street. He avoided the cowboys and their horses as he tried to cut a straight and true course towards the marshal's office. He moved around a buckboard and mounted the boardwalk. With every step he took Sanders glanced across the street and focused on the Lucky Dollar.

As his fear increased, so did his pace. Sanders walked quickly for a man with a belly and reached the marshal's office in a matter of only minutes.

NINE

Matt Fallen looked up as the door of his office flew open and a sweat-soaked Doyle Sanders entered. The burly saloon owner pulled his coat tails free of the door as he closed it, then hurried to pull down the blind as though he feared anyone seeing him in the office. The lawman buttoned his fresh shirt and tucked it into his pants. He watched as Sanders peeped around the lowered blind. Fallen plucked his tin star from his bloodstained leather vest and pinned it to his shirt.

The lawman could not conceal his curiosity.

'Anything I can do for you, Sanders?' he asked, resting a hip on the edge of his desk and looking at his unexpected visitor.

Sanders was panting like a hound dog as he glanced across the office at the marshal.

'Something's going on in War Smoke, Marshal,' Sanders said in a flurry of words. 'I don't know what, but I've got a very bad feeling about it.'

Fallen tilted his head and studied the man. He had never seen Sanders look anything except cool, calm and collected before. Now the saloon owner was sweating like a pig and looked terrified. The lawman wondered what could have caused such a change in the businessman's usual composure.

'Calm down, Sanders,' the marshal advised. 'You look fit to burst. Tell me what's got you so all fired up.'

Sanders moved closer to the tall lawman. 'Bob King paid me a visit a few minutes back and told me that there's a rumour going around town that there are hired gunmen in War Smoke and I'm the one who hired them.'

'Did you hire a couple of gunmen, Sanders?' Fallen asked. He watched the face of the owner of the Longhorn carefully.

'Certainly not, Marshal.' Sanders mopped his brow, then continued: 'I've never hired gunmen.'

'Then forget about it,' Matt Fallen told him. He smiled. 'Let the rumours settle. They'll go away in time.'

'You don't understand, Fallen,' Sanders said. 'Let me explain and then you might understand why I'm so jittery.'

Matt Fallen shrugged. 'I'm listening.'

Sanders nodded and took a breath to calm his frazzled nerves. 'I was making my way here when I saw Bob King talking with a stranger. A stranger with a pretty handsome shooting rig.'

Fallen raised his eyebrows.

'That's interesting,' he drawled. 'Carry on.'

'King paid the stranger a lot of money,' Sanders told him.

Fallen ran a thumb along his jaw. 'So King tells you that there happens to be a rumour that you've hired a paid gunman and then you see him handing over cash to a stranger who looks like a hired gunman. Right?'

'Exactly right, Marshal.' Sanders nodded. 'Can you understand my agitation?'

'I think I can, Sanders.' Fallen nodded.

'Is it true that someone was killed in town earlier, Marshal?' Sanders wondered. 'Is it?'

Matt Fallen nodded slowly. 'Yep, it is. Old Joel

Erikson got his head blown off in the alleyway behind the stagecoach livery.'

Sanders looked shocked by the information.

'Good grief!'

'I've bin scratching my head trying to figure out who would want to kill old Joel but so far I've come up empty. That old man didn't have any enemies that I know about.' The marshal sighed. 'But somebody still killed him, all the same.'

Sanders mopped his face again.

'You don't think that someone might be planning to rob me of the prize money, do you?' Sanders asked. 'Maybe Joel was killed as a sort of distraction.'

'Maybe.' Matt Fallen rubbed his jaw again thoughtfully. 'This might have something to do with the big poker game you've organized, I guess. You've put up a mighty large sum of money and that might be a motive.'

Sanders sat down on the hardback chair beside Fallen. 'I don't understand any of this, but you might be right. Why would anyone kill Joel? Why would someone say that I've hired killers? Can you make any sense of it?'

Fallen shook his head. 'I'm as confused as you are, Sanders. All I know is that we have us a lot of strangers in War Smoke and at least one of them is a known killer. I'm reliably informed Travis Grey is in town.'

Sanders looked like a scared jackrabbit.

'The locobean?' he gasped.

'Yep.' Fallen nodded. 'Trouble is that it ain't illegal to be crazy as long as you don't get caught.'

'Maybe he killed old Joel,' Sanders ventured.

'Impossible,' Fallen said regretfully. 'Joel was killed a long time before Grey even got here. So there has to be more than one killer in War Smoke.'

Sanders looked like a man who has just had every drop of blood drained from his face. He was pale and trembling as he sat next to the marshal.

'What have I done?' he muttered.

Fallen looked down at the troubled saloon owner. 'What do you mean by that, Sanders? You ain't done nothing as far I know.'

Doyle Sanders looked up at the lawman. 'It's all my fault, Marshal. I put ads in a dozen newspapers about the big poker game I'm staging. I've drawn the scum from every corner of the territory here.'

Matt Fallen sighed. 'I reckon someone is just using the poker game as a cover to hide whatever it is they're really intending to do. With so many gamblers in town it's darn hard picking out all the extra faces.'

Sanders looked at the lawman. 'King said that there are rumours around town that the banker and even you are targets for the hired gunmen, Fallen.'

Matt Fallen brooded on the words.

'It wouldn't be the first time that someone's hired a gunfighter to draw down on me, Sanders.' He smiled. 'But then I do kinda upset a lot of folks.'

The saloon owner was losing his battle to stanch the flow of sweat which covered his face. His troubled eyes glanced at the lawman.

'Am I in danger, Marshal?' he wondered.

'Maybe you are, Sanders,' the marshal said as he pondered the few facts they actually knew. 'Maybe we both are and more than one gunman has been paid to kill more than one victim in War Smoke. Like you said, this might all be a distraction so that someone can steal the prize money. We'll find out soon enough, though.'

'What should I d-do?' Sanders stammered.

'Wish I knew the answer to that, Sanders,' Fallen said. 'But I still ain't figured out why someone killed old Joel yet.'

'Do you think that I should I hire myself a few guards to protect the prize money, Marshal?' Sanders asked.

'Where are you keeping the prize money at the moment?' Fallen queried.

'I've got it all in my safe at the Longhorn.'

Matt Fallen tilted his head. 'I reckon a few guards might be good insurance against any would-be robbers, Sanders,' he advised.

The saloon owner was about to answer when the office door suddenly flew open. Sanders gasped while Matt Fallen drew his Peacemaker and cocked its hammer in one swift action.

Startled, Elmer looked innocently at the two men and slowly grinned as he tentatively entered the office. Without taking his eyes off the marshal or Sanders the deputy made his way to the stove.

'Quit horsing around, Marshal Fallen,' he said, chuckling. Using a cloth he lifted the coffee pot off the hot stove. 'I only come here to make you some special coffee.'

Fallen watched as Elmer prepared his various ingredients to be added to the pot. Then he helped Sanders up from his chair.

'C'mon, Sanders. I'll walk you back to the Longhorn,' Fallen said, placing his Stetson on his head. The two men headed for the office door and left the deputy feverishly working like a demented witch over a cauldron.

As the pair weaved their way through the traffic and crossed Front Street, Matt Fallen slowed his pace.

'What's wrong, Marshal?' Sanders asked the lawman.

Fallen said nothing as he studied the black roan with the white stockings. His eyes just wandered over the animal, which was still tethered to the hitching pole.

'That's a mighty fine piece of horseflesh, Marshal,' Sanders remarked.

'It sure is.' Matt Fallen nodded. Then he continued to escort Sanders towards the Longhorn saloon.

TEN

News of the commotion in which Joel Erikson had been brutally killed had travelled like wildfire through the streets of War Smoke. It reached the veteran medical man as he sat outside his small office on a hardback chair. Doc Weaver listened to the gossip with interest for a few moments, then he struck a match and lit his pipe.

Smoke hung over the medical man as he succumbed to his curiosity. He rose to his feet and walked towards the heart of the sprawling settlement. The wily old medical man was well aware that such stories had a tendency to become exaggerated the more people passed from one to another. Doc wanted to find out the truth for himself and that meant heading to the source.

The town's many streetlights and lanterns glimmered in the darkness, but nightfall did not seem to trouble any of the inhabitants of War Smoke. The darker it got the livelier the town became as they defied nature and continued to go about their business.

Doc Weaver ambled into the funeral parlour with his pipe gripped firmly in his mouth. A series of small smoke clouds marked his trail across the well-furnished front office to a heavy drape that hung from the wall. Doc pulled the hefty curtain aside and peered into the business part of the undertaker's premises. Unlike the parlour at the front, the place where the work was done was drab and cold.

Crude coffins stood against the wall, waiting to be filled, whilst two marble slabs lay upon solid oak tables. Doc looked through his pipe smoke at one of the slabs: the one with the body of Joel Erikson resting upon its smooth surface.

Abe Sims looked up from his latest client.

'Howdy, Doc,' he greeted Weaver.

Doc came further into the back room and stared at the brutally murdered man. He rubbed his whiskers and slowly moved around the corpse. He sniffed and glanced at the undertaker.

'I heard that this used to be old Joel Erikson, Abe,' he said. 'Hard to tell who it is with most of his head turned to a bloody pulp like this.'

'Yeah, he sure don't look his best, Doc.' Abe Sims shook his head. He opened a drawer and produced a bottle of whiskey. 'I was about to strip and wash him down when you showed up. You want a snort, Doc?'

'I'd be grateful.' Doc accepted the bottle and put its neck to his lips. The fiery liquid burned a trail down his throat as he handed the whiskey back to the undertaker.

Sims took a swig, then placed the bottle on the desk. He moved to the carcass and frowned.

'I always have me a nip of the hard stuff when I've gotta tackle something like this, Doc,' he admitted.

'I figured as much.' Doc puffed on his pipe and inspected the clothing carefully. He pulled out a blood-soaked wallet from the inside pocket of the body's coat and opened it. 'I come over here to give you a hand.'

'Mighty grateful, Doc.' Abe filled a bucket with water from a kettle and placed it on the edge of the slab. 'Matt Fallen figured it was old Joel by an engraving inside his pocket watch.'

'I put three stitches in his left hand a couple of years back, Abe.' Doc pointed his pipe at the hand. 'It's Joel right enough.'

Sims looked grimly at the task before him. 'In forty years I ain't never felt sick before, but this is just horrific. Only a monster would do this sort of thing, Doc.'

'It's kinda strange when you think about it, Abe,' Weaver observed as he held the sticky wallet in his hands. 'Someone fires both barrels of a scattergun at a man's face as if he didn't want it identified, but he leaves him with a watch and wallet which makes identification easy. It don't add up.'

Sims rubbed his bald pate. 'There must be a madman in town, Doc. Nobody is safe.'

Doc nodded as he carefully pulled the wallet's leather pockets apart to reveal its contents. He stared at the banknotes in the wallet and looked up at Sims.

'This poor critter weren't robbed, Abe,' he said. 'He's got quite a bit of cash in here.'

'How much money is in there, Doc?' Sims asked.

Doc extracted four bills and set them down on the marble slab carefully. A twenty and three hundred-dollar bills only added to the mystery.

'Well, look at this, Abe,' Doc said as he separated one of the banknotes and showed it to the undertaker. 'This is a half of a torn hundred-dollar bill.'

Abe Sims walked round the slab and stared at the segment of the banknote held between Doc's fingers.

'Well, I'll be!' Sims gasped. 'That is a hundred-dollar bill right enough. Leastways, it's half of one.'

Doc nodded. 'The half with no serial numbers on it.'

'What's that mean?'

'It means this is useless unless it gets together with the other half of the bill, Abe,' Doc told him. He searched inside the wallet again.

'What you looking for, Doc?' Sims asked, leaning over the shorter man.

'This,' Doc said. He pulled out a note and squinted at the words scrawled in pencil upon it. He moved under the overhead lantern and nodded. 'This is what got Joel killed, Abe. This note and the hundred-dollar bill were bait for Joel and he got himself hooked.'

'What's it say?' the undertaker asked, curious to know.

'I'll tell you later, Abe.' Doc pushed the torn bill and the note into his coat pocket and walked to the drape. As he pulled the curtain away he looked over his shoulder at the confused undertaker. 'I'm going to find Matt. This note explains why old Joel was in the alley behind the stagecoach livery.'

'It does?'

'It sure does, Abe.' Doc moved swiftly and left the funeral parlour. The small clouds of pipe smoke hung in the air long after his departure.

Abe Sims scratched his bald head and sighed heavily. He turned and looked at the body. His eyes then focused on the undamaged banknotes on the slab.

The undertaker smiled and slyly pocketed the money.

ELEVEN

The two drifters had consumed most of the contents of their whiskey bottle. They staggered out of the saloon into the fresh evening air and leaned against the porch uprights. Akins toyed with his guns as his partner watched the busy boardwalk through blurred eyes.

'We oughta get us a room, Frank,' Poole said. 'I'm tuckered out.'

'I ain't tired, Sam,' Akins snarled. 'I'm for us finding our benefactor and learning what he wants us to do.'

Sam Poole sighed. Then he saw the broad-shouldered stranger moving through the crowd towards them. Draped in a long trail coat which was pushed over a holstered gun the stranger approached the two drunken drifters confidently. For a moment Poole did not say anything, then he realized that the stranger was heading straight for them.

Poole steadied himself and patted his saddle pal's shoulder frantically.

'Look, Frank,' he warned.

Akins spat at the ground, then raised his head and glared at the stranger. His flexed fingers hovered above his gun grips.

'I see him, Sam,' Akins growled.

Undaunted, the stranger continued his advance and stopped three feet from them. His eyes darted between the drifters as he chewed on a toothpick.

'Are you boys known as Akins and Poole?' he asked.

Poole nodded nervously. 'We are. Who the hell are you?'

'I've bin sent to round you boys up,' the stranger drawled.

Frank Akins's faced twitched. He was unused to anyone having the guts to face him the way this unknown man was doing.

'We ain't going anywhere with you, stranger,' the drifter growled.

The stranger raised an eyebrow.

'Why not?' His tone was mocking. 'I didn't figure on you boys being scared.'

His words were like a match to Akins's fuse. The drifter erupted in fury, grabbed the stranger's bandanna and was about to drag the man towards him when he felt the barrel of a gun being pushed into his belly. Akins looked down at the gleaming six-shooter. He released the bandanna and backed away.

'Who are you, stranger?' he asked.

'It don't matter none,' the unblinking stranger said calmly, moving the toothpick between his lips. 'All you gotta do is come with me to earn your blood money.'

Poole moved to Akins's side but looked at the stranger as his trembling voice asked, 'Now?'

'Now,' the stranger insisted. He slipped his gun back into its holster. He curled his finger. 'Follow me.'

'Where we going?' Akins asked.

'To meet the boss,' the stranger replied.

Akins tried to look as confident as the man who had already given proof of his speed with a gun.

'What's the hurry?'

'You've got work to do,' the stranger said.

'Tonight?' Akins frowned in disbelief.

The stranger nodded. 'Yep. Tonight.'

The drifters followed the stranger like lambs obediently trailing a ewe. The three men were soon enveloped in a sea of other strangers.

The sound of tinny pianos drifted from the many saloons, filling the crowded streets of War Smoke with melodic music.

Soon another noise would silence them.

TWELVE

Doc Weaver pushed the swing doors apart and entered the Longhorn saloon. The short medical man had never seen so many people crammed into such a narrow room before. The odour of sweat mingled with the mouth-drying fumes of coal tar lanterns in the long bar-room. As Doc forced his way through the crowd he relied on memory rather than sight. All he could see were the shoulders, backs and chests of men as they filled every square inch of floor space.

Doc had walked to the marshal's office after leaving the funeral parlour, but was then told that Matt Fallen had walked to the Longhorn with Doyle Sanders. Although Doc had no idea why the lawman had gone with the saloon owner he had wasted very little time in his pursuit of Fallen.

After a valiant struggle Doc reached the bar counter and pushed two men apart in order to get the attention of one of the bartenders. He signalled to the thin man to come closer.

'What'll it be, Doc?' the bartender shouted over the noise.

'Where's the marshal?' Doc shouted back.

'I ain't seen him, Doc,' the bartender replied, He pointed to the rear of the big room. 'If he's here he might be at the back with Doyle.'

'Much obliged,' Doc yelled. He pushed his way through the crowd. There were few men who were as determined as he. The Longhorn was so overcrowded that when one man moved everybody moved. Doc felt a surge and found himself pressed up against the side wall for a few moments.

After muttering some curses the doctor ducked under a few arms and managed to turn himself away from the wall. He straightened his old hat, raised his hands in an attempt to claw his way to the back door and used every ounce of his strength to force his way through the crowd.

Once again Doc was relying on instinct, for he could not see anything apart from unyielding torsos. As the small man was buffeted by the press of bodies he felt something soft in the palms of his hands. Doc squinted as he was pushed closer to the handsome dance-hall girl.

He blinked and looked up into the painted face of a smiling female; then he realized that he was clutching her ample bosom.

He blushed slightly as his nostrils were filled with her perfume.

'Well howdy, Clara,' he stammered.

'Why, Doc,' she cooed gratefully as she traced his jawbone with a finger. 'Ain't you the frisky one?'

Doc blinked hard and withdrew his hands from her breasts as he was pushed even closer into her. Always the gentleman Doc carefully pulled away from her fragrant charms and raised his hat.

'My apologies, Clara.' He cleared his throat and then felt fingers returning the favour. 'I hope that was an accident, gal.'

She winked at him.

Doc continued on towards the back of the saloon. He looked over his shoulder and shouted back to her. 'Don't fret, Clara. This ain't a house call. There won't be any charge.'

Exhausted, Doc reached the door at last.

Ignoring the sign with the word PRIVATE painted upon it he rattled the handle and pushed the door open.

He sighed heavily as he closed the door behind him and glanced along the dimly lit corridor. He scratched a match and lit his pipe. The brief glow from the match flame showed him where Sanders's office was.

Doc shook out the flame on the match, walked to the door and rapped upon it with his knuckles.

'You in there, Matt?' he shouted.

The door opened wide and Fallen stood there like a great tree between Doc and the seated figure of Doyle Sanders.

'What are you doing here, Doc?' Fallen asked his pipe-smoking friend.

'I came here to give you something mighty important, Matt.' Doc waved the marshal out of the way and walked to the centre of the office. He glanced at the tomes lining the wall and nodded to Sanders, who was seated behind the desk, as his fingers searched his coat pocket.

'Something important?' Fallen repeated.

'That's what I said, didn't I?' Doc muttered. He began to empty the contents of his pocket on to Sanders's desk.

Matt Fallen closed the office door and followed Doc to the desk. He pushed his hat back on his head and watched as the elderly doctor placed handfuls of litter on top of Sanders's ink blotter.

'What are you doing, Doc?' Fallen asked.

'Patience, Matt.' Doc surveyed the blotter and found what he was searching for. He picked up the torn hundred-dollar bill and the note he had taken from the dead man's wallet. He gave them to the lawman. 'Here.'

Fallen eyed the note and the torn bill in his hands.

'Where'd you get these, Doc?' the lawman asked.

'I found them on old Joel's body in the funeral parlour, Matt,' Doc replied. 'I think you'll find them mighty interesting.'

Fallen studied what was in his hands carefully.

Sanders rose from his chair and stared at the tall lawman. He moved to Weaver's side and looked at the ripped bank bill and note in the marshal's hands.

'You did a good job finding this, Doc,' Fallen told his old friend. 'I didn't think to search the body after I saw his name engraved inside the pocket watch.'

Sanders pointed at the scrap of paper. 'What is that, Marshal?'

'It's a note claiming to be from Bob King, Sanders,' he drawled. 'It asks Joel to meet him in the alley behind the livery. That's where I found his blood-soaked body.'

'Bob King.' Sanders nodded and grabbed the note from Fallen's hands. 'I knew it was him behind this.'

Matt Fallen and Doc watched as the smile vanished from the saloon owner's face. Sanders looked up at the marshal and gave him back the note.

'This is not Bob's handwriting, Marshal,' he declared.

'It ain't?' Doc gasped.

'Are you sure, Sanders?' Fallen asked. 'It's signed Bob King.'

Doyle Sanders sat down and shook his head.

'I'm dead sure, Marshal,' he said. 'Whoever wrote that note to lure old Joel to his death, it was not Bob King. I know his handwriting well.'

Matt Fallen let out a long breath and placed the torn bill and note in his shirt pocket. He looked at the faces of both men in turn. They were as bewildered as he was.

'I've still got a gut feeling that this has something to do with the poker tournament, Sanders,' Fallen said. 'At least, it has something to do with that prize money you've got in your safe.'

Doc scratched his whiskers. 'I suggest you take that money to the jail, Matt. You could lock it up in one of your cells. It should be safer there than here.'

'That's a good idea, Doc.' Fallen nodded. 'If Mr Sanders here agrees, that's exactly what I intend doing.'

Before any words could leave Sanders's lips the office shook once again as the deafening thunder of shotgun blasts resonated throughout War Smoke.

The three men stared at one another in disbelief.

'What was that?' Sanders swung round and stared at the barred window of his office.

'That was a scattergun,' Doc opined.

Marshal Matt Fallen shook his head.

'You're wrong, Doc,' he disagreed. 'That was the sound of twin-barrelled death.'

THIRTEEN

The telling aroma of gunsmoke hung in the evening air as Matt Fallen led Doc from the side door of the Longhorn and moved silently along the alley towards Front Street. Fallen slowed his determined pace and paused when he reached the corner of the saloon. His narrowed eyes surveyed the still, busy thoroughfare carefully as men and women passed by. The sound that had drawn Fallen and Doc from the saloon into the night had died away but the lawman was not deterred. He knew that the acrid scent of buckshot would tell him where the shooting had come from.

Doc peered round the marshal's arm.

'Where'd you reckon them shots came from, Matt?' he asked.

For some moments Matt Fallen studied the people who still crowded the boardwalks; then he raised a finger and pointed.

'From over there,' he answered firmly.

Bewildered, Doc looked at the tall lawman.

'How can you tell, Matt?' Doc asked. 'How can you be so sure?'

Matt Fallen stared into the lantern-lit street.

'It's easy when you know what to look for, Doc,' he said.

'It is?'

'Yep, it is.' The lawman left the cover of the alley and marched across the street towards the Diamond Pin Hotel with his companion at his side. Lantern light gleamed from every door and window and spread across their path.

'How come we're headed this way, Matt?'

'Because this is the right way, Doc,' Fallen insisted.

'How can you tell?' Doc growled.

As they reached the hotel porch Fallen paused and glanced all around them. He pointed at the other people in the street, then leaned down and whispered in the shorter man's ear.

'Think about it. This is the one place that everyone is walking away from, Doc,' he explained. 'It

117

stands to reason that the sound of the gunshots came from here. Most folks are like wild critters, Doc. They run away from loud noises.'

Doc scratched the back of his head. 'I reckon so.'

Fallen looked at the buildings on either side of the alley. He patted his companion's shoulder.

'Follow me,' he said.

Both men made their way up between the hotel and the general store. Fallen raised a hand and stopped the older man in his tracks. Doc remained in the lawman's shadow as Fallen again caught the scent of gunsmoke on the cool breeze.

It was far stronger at the rear of the buildings. The marshal glanced into the blackest of shadows. There were vague outlines of buildings adjoining the hotel, he thought. They did not permit the moonlight to reach the ground.

The marshal was about to walk towards the darkness when he heard the sound of footsteps. No matter how hard he tried, Fallen was unable to see the man he could hear advancing towards him and the elderly doctor.

'You carrying a gun, Doc?' Fallen whispered to his friend.

Doc was surprised by the question.

'You know that I never carry any weapons, Matt,' he answered.

The marshal's mind raced. He knew that Weaver could never outrun a bullet. He briefly glanced at his friend.

'Get yourself behind something, Doc,' he advised.

Fallen bit his lower lip and returned his attention to the sound of footsteps moving ever closer in the shadows. His heart was racing as he focused his eyes into the eerie blackness.

'Who is that?' Fallen called out, his hand hovering a few inches above his holstered Peacemaker. 'Identify yourself.'

The footsteps defiantly continued to get louder. The lawman knew that whoever was hidden by the shadows was unafraid. That meant he was either very brave or he was totally insane.

Not even the most daring of gunfighters would approach like this, he told himself.

Then suddenly Fallen saw the figure walk into the moonlight from the depths of the shadows. The lawman squinted hard at the well-armed creature. The light of the moon illuminated the two guns that the man wore across his waist.

Fallen flexed his fingers over his gun grip.

'Who are you?'

There was no reply. The man stopped not more than ten feet away from the marshal and glared at him from under his hat brim.

Fallen could feel the fight which was about to happen.

'Get down, Doc,' he ordered his old friend without taking his eyes off the gunman.

The elderly doctor did exactly as he was told and knelt behind a water barrel. He did not utter a word as the lawman slowly ventured closer to his silent adversary.

Fallen had taken only one step when the man drew one of his six-shooters and fanned its hammer unexpectedly. A red flame cut through the moonlight and knocked the lawman off his feet. The marshal landed heavily on his back.

Matt Fallen was about to move when he felt a pain high in his shoulder. His head turned and he saw blood covering his fresh shirt.

The wounded marshal scrambled to his feet faster than he had hit the ground. He glared through the smoke which still drifted from the gun barrel in the man's hand.

'Who are you?' Fallen asked, He could feel

blood trickling down the length of one arm, spreading between his fingers.

The man tilted his head back. 'Travis Grey.'

'So you're Travis Grey?' Fallen said.

'They told me you were as big as a tree,' Travis Grey remarked as he pulled back on his gun hammer again. 'They were right, Marshal. You are as big as a tree but, like I told them, there ain't nothing I like better than felling trees.'

Before the marshal could respond a blinding streak of lethal lead spewed from the gun barrel again. The marshal twisted on his heels and once more he was sent crashing to the ground.

Fallen just lay there, motionless.

Doc squinted hard from behind the barrel.

'Are you OK, Matt?' he desperately called.

There was no answer.

Doc was about to go to where Fallen lay when he saw Travis Grey moving through the hazy smoke towards his helpless victim. Grey still held his six-shooter in his hand.

It was still aimed at the marshal on the ground.

Doc watched as the gunman trained his still-smoking weapon on the prostrate lawman and pulled back on its hammer until it had fully locked.

Even though Doc was unarmed he jumped to his feet and screamed out across the distance between himself and Grey.

'You stinking yella bastard.'

Startled, Grey looked up from his intended target and raised his six-shooter at Doc. Without warning Fallen brought his boot up and kicked Grey in his groin. As the madman buckled the marshal grabbed Grey's gun hand and wrestled him to the ground.

The gun fired another deafening shot. A flash of lightning passed within inches of the lawman as he dragged Grey off his feet. The lawman blocked a clubbing left hand and then smashed a clenched fist across his foe's jaw.

Travis Grey went head over heels and landed on his back.

Stunned and bleeding, Fallen forced himself on to one knee and glared at Grey. To his horror the lawman saw the moonlight glance across the six-shooter in his opponent's hand; then he heard its hammer being cocked.

Knowing his life was hanging by a thread Fallen feverishly drew his Peacemaker and fanned its hammer at Grey. The venomous shot cut through the moonlight into its target.

A plume of blood erupted from Grey's chest.

The gunman fell lifelessly on to his face.

'You got him, Matt!' Doc shouted, and ran from behind the barrel to the wounded marshal. 'You got that crazy back-shooter.'

Fallen allowed Doc to help him back to his feet and unsteadily moved towards the dead man. He used his boot to turn the body on to his back, then he stared down at his face.

'Who is he, Matt?'

With blood trailing down his face Fallen sighed and pushed his gun back into his holster.

'Travis Grey,' he muttered. 'He must have come here to chop me down, Doc. The runt nearly did.'

Doc was fussing around the tall lawman as Fallen turned and walked to where Grey had emerged from. Something was gnawing at his craw.

'I'd best get you to my office, Matt,' Doc said as the lawman continued to stride into the shadows. 'I have to see how bad you're wounded.'

'Hold on, Doc,' Fallen said, continuing to walk into the darkness of the hotel's outbuildings. 'I gotta check something out.'

Doc trailed the tall lawman. 'What are you doing, Matt? Your job's done. You shot the maniac

123

that's bin going around town killing folks. Come with me so I can check out your wounds.'

Matt Fallen did not utter a word until he found what he had been searching for in the shadows. He stopped, turned and glanced at Doc.

'Two more bodies, Doc.' He sighed. 'Check them out for me, will you?'

Doc went to where the marshal was indicating and knelt between the two dead men.

'They look like a couple of drifters to me, Matt,' he said. 'They've bin blasted with a scattergun.'

Fallen stood over the bodies and stared down at what was left of the two men.

'Just like I feared. Looks like we've still got ourselves a killer to find, Doc.' The marshal sighed and looked back at Travis Grey.

Doc got back to his feet and looked puzzled.

'But you just shot the varmint that killed these two critters, Matt,' he said, pointing at Grey's body. 'Ain't that him?'

Fallen shook his head. 'Travis Grey was a madman and must have wanted me dead for some reason, but he didn't kill those two drifters, Doc. You just told me they were shot with a scattergun. Travis only ever used his six-shooters.'

'I don't understand,' Doc admitted. 'Grey came

from where them bodies are spread out, Matt.'

'I figure the real killer high-tailed it before Travis even showed up,' Fallen reasoned. 'We're looking for a man who can move around War Smoke virtually unnoticed with a scattergun hidden on him. He must wear a long dustcoat of some kind. Long enough to conceal a twin-barrelled shotgun.'

Doc did not bother to argue with his wounded friend. He just nodded and then allowed the towering lawman to use him as a crutch. He led him back down to the busy street.

'We're going to my office not yours, Doc,' Fallen announced as they turned the corner into Front Street. 'You can tend my wounds there. I reckon I'm only winged anyway.'

Doc looked exasperated. 'You're a stubborn varmint, Matt Fallen,' he said.

FOURTEEN

Asa Fenton and his brother Olin had waited for hours in the large suite at the Diamond Pin Hotel. They had heard and ignored the shootings that had rocked War Smoke, in anticipation of their client's arrival. It was nearly midnight before a knock on the door drew their attention.

Olin moved to behind the door and pulled his gun from his shoulder holster as his brother went to answer.

Both the Fentons looked at one another. Olin nodded. Asa turned the knob and opened the door.

'I'm looking for the Fenton brothers.'

'You found them,' Asa said.

'I only see one.'

Asa smiled. 'My brother has his gun aimed at you.'

'May I come in?'

'We've no objections.' Asa nodded. 'Come on in.'

Olin Fenton closed the door as both he and Asa watched the unfamiliar man enter the room. Bob King sat down on the edge of one of the two identical beds and watched as the well-dressed siblings moved around the room like a pair of caged mountain lions.

'This has to be done perfectly, boys,' King said, staring at the floor. 'By that I mean there ain't no room for mistakes.'

'We don't make mistakes,' Olin said, toying with his gun and watching the saloon owner.

'I'm glad about that.' King nodded.

Asa moved closer to their paymaster. 'Exactly who do you want killed?'

'You come straight to the point, don't you?'

Olin Fenton sat opposite the saloon owner and watched him like a hawk. 'Me and Asa heard a lot of gunplay earlier. What was that all about? Anything we ought to be told about?'

'Nothing for you boys to trouble yourselves

over,' King said with a smile. 'Just a few drunken cowboys tangling with the marshal, I'm told.'

'Who do you want us to kill?' Asa asked again.

'Just a worthless critter named Mort Heely.' King watched the two men carefully. 'He happens to own the bank in War Smoke.'

Olin Fenton narrowed his stare. 'Me and my brother don't rob banks. If that's what you're intending then you best hire yourselves someone else.'

King smiled. 'I don't want to rob the bank, boys. I just want the owner of the only bank in town killed. It's a simple business.'

Asa and Olin looked at each other, then returned their full attention to King.

'I don't get it,' Asa admitted.

'Me neither,' Olin added with a shrug.

King stood and donned his hat. 'You don't have to understand anything, boys. You just have to kill Mort Heely for me.'

Both brothers stood between King and the door of the room.

'Why do you want this critter dead?' Olin asked.

'My brother's curious,' Asa added with a smile. 'Olin don't like being curious. He can get damn ornery when he's curious.'

King looked at Olin. 'Is that right?'

'Yep. You wouldn't like me when I'm curious,' Olin said. He toyed with his gun. 'Why do you want us to kill Mort Heely?'

King shuffled his feet. 'When he's dead I can buy his bank for a fraction of its value. Satisfied?'

Asa held out his hand.

'When we get our fee we'll be satisfied,' he said.

Bob King pulled his wallet from the inside pocket of his coat and opened its flap. He peeled off four bills and placed them on the palm of Asa's hand.

'OK?' King asked.

Both siblings nodded.

'When do you want it done?' Asa asked as he pocketed the cash.

'Tonight,' King answered. He handed a small scrap of paper to Olin. 'That's his address.'

Olin looked at the paper and then handed it to his brother.

'What does Mort Heely look like?' he asked.

'Old,' King said. 'Real old.'

Asa and Olin both smiled.

'He'll be dead before sunup,' Olin said, opening the door. 'Nice doing business with you.'

Bob King walked out of the room. As he

strolled down the long corridor towards the top of the hotel staircase he smiled broadly.

His plan was taking shape.

FIFTEEN

Elmer looked in horror at the sight of Matt Fallen as he was helped into the marshal's office by the slight figure of Doc Weaver. The deputy guided the wounded lawman to a cot. Fallen lay down upon it as Doc checked the wounds. Elmer looked on, feeling more than helpless.

'Glory be, Marshal Fallen. You done plumb ruined that new shirt,' he said. 'I'll get you some coffee.'

Doc turned his head. 'I'll have me a cup as well, Elmer.'

Fallen looked at his old friend. 'Are you loco?'

'Easy, Matt,' Doc said as he checked the wounds. 'You're lucky. Both shots just grazed you.'

'Then stop the bleeding so I can get back on my feet and get back out there,' Fallen said. 'That killer is still on the loose and I intend stopping him from killing anyone else.'

'This might hurt.' Doc pulled a small bottle of iodine from his coat pocket and carefully dabbed it against the marshal's grazed temple.

Elmer handed them both two tin cups full of his specially brewed beverage.

'Drink it down,' the deputy urged. 'Them Chinese herbs will do you both good.'

Doc took a mouthful of the coffee. 'That ain't half bad, Elmer boy.'

Fallen tasted the coffee and, to his surprise, liked it. He downed the entire contents of his cup.

'Damn it all, Elmer. Why can't you make coffee that good every day?' he asked.

'How come you got yourself shot up, Marshal Fallen?' Elmer responded with another question as he carried the empty cups back to the stove.

Fallen sat up on the cot and pushed the saw-bones aside.

'I ain't finished, Matt,' Doc protested.

'Yes you are.' Fallen stood and walked to his desk. He sat down and stared at the circulars in front of him. Suddenly his expression altered as he lifted the top Wanted poster. 'The black roan with white stockings.'

Elmer and Doc looked at the marshal.

'What about it, Matt?' Doc asked as he refilled his cup.

'You don't understand,' Fallen said. 'I've bin trying to figure out why that horse was important and it's here on this poster. Frank Akins, wanted dead or alive for murder. Known to ride a black roan with white stockings.'

'Is he in town, Marshal Fallen?' Elmer wondered.

'He's lying dead behind the Diamond Pin with his saddle pal and Travis Grey,' the lawman replied.

'I'd better go wake up Abe Sims,' Elmer said, and shrugged.

Fallen stood and plucked his bloodstained vest off the back of his chair. He put it on and pointed at Doc.

'You go tell Abe, Doc,' he said.

'What are you intending doing, Matt?' asked Doc. He finished his coffee and placed the cup on top of the stove.

'Me and Elmer are going back to Doyle Sanders at the Longhorn,' Fallen told him. 'I've gotta bring his prize money over here for safe keeping like I promised.'

Elmer grinned. 'Miss Clara works in the Longhorn.'

Doc recalled his earlier encounter with the buxom Clara and cleared his throat. 'I'll head on over to the funeral parlour and tell Abe he's got three new customers.'

Elmer watched as Doc hurried out of the office.

'I ain't never seen Doc move that fast before, Marshal Fallen,' he said, adjusting his gunbelt. 'I reckon it must be my coffee.'

Matt Fallen stared through the window at the scores of people who were still defying his wall clock. The marshal touched his tender scalp and gritted his teeth. He tossed a set of keys to his deputy.

'Get yourself a shotgun, Elmer. I've a feeling you might need it.'

Elmer moved to the rifle rack and opened the padlock on the chain that was securing the array of weapons to the wall. He pulled a rifle free and placed it on the desk.

'Do you want me to get you one, Marshal Fallen?' he asked the lawman, who was checking his Peacemaker.

Fallen glanced at his young deputy and slipped his gun back into its holster.

'I'm fine, Elmer,' Fallen told his underling. 'You'd best get your pockets full of shells for that cannon.'

Elmer emptied a box of shotgun cartridges on to the desk and crammed as many as he could fit into his pockets. He then returned the keys to Fallen and followed him out on to the boardwalk. The lofty lawman locked the office door and turned to face the street.

'How are you figuring to catch the killer, Marshal Fallen?' Elmer asked. He was struggling with the hefty double-barrelled weapon. 'We don't know who he is or where he is. Come to think about it, we don't know nothing.'

'I don't figure on us chasing shadows all over War Smoke, Elmer,' the marshal replied. 'I intend him to come looking for us.'

'Come again?'

'I still reckon all these killings have something to do with the massive prize money Sanders has promised to pay the winner of the poker tournament, Elmer,' Fallen said as he studied the unusually busy street. 'I intend locking that cash up in our jail.'

Elmer grinned and tapped the side of his nose. 'And then that varmint will come here looking for it. The murderous critter will give himself away.'

'Something like that, Elmer.'

Matt Fallen looked across at the Longhorn. Unlike the rest of the saloons along Front Street it was far busier than either of the star-packers had ever seen before.

'Them folks are spilling out into the street from the Longhorn, Marshal Fallen,' Elmer said as he trailed the tall lawman towards the saloon. 'I don't reckon we could even get to the bar counter, let alone find old Sanders.'

Fallen rested his hand on his holstered gun.

'We're going in through the side door,' he said.

'That's a mercy.' Elmer followed the marshal round the line of horses tied to the hitching poles and up into the dark alley. The deputy watched as Fallen opened the side door, then he tracked the marshal along the corridor to Sanders's office.

Fallen knocked on the door.

'It's Marshal Fallen, Sanders,' he shouted. 'Open up.'

There was no response. Both lawmen looked at one another for a few moments.

'Maybe he ain't in there, Marshal Fallen,'

Elmer suggested. 'He might be in the saloon getting himself a drink.'

Fallen grabbed the doorknob and turned it. 'It ain't locked, Elmer.'

The marshal entered Sanders's private domain and stopped in his tracks. The office was shrouded in darkness. The only light was that which managed to come in through the barred window.

'He must have gone someplace,' the deputy suggested.

Matt Fallen inhaled deeply. He looked at his deputy.

'Do you smell that?' he asked.

Elmer sniffed the air. 'Gunsmoke.'

Matt Fallen crossed the room to the desk and stopped next to the lamp. He pulled out a box of matches from his pocket and withdrew one. Elmer watched as the marshal scratched it with a thumbnail and touched the lamp's wick.

The room suddenly lit up.

'Glory be!' Elmer gasped.

Matt Fallen stared at Doyle Sanders's crumpled body lying on the floor between his chair and desk. The marshal knelt and pulled the saloon owner on to his back. Sanders had been killed neatly, unlike the other bodies Fallen had come across earlier.

A single bullet hole in the shirtfront indicated all that had been needed to kill Sanders. Fallen ripped the shirtfront apart and stared at the bloody chest.

He rose back up to his full height.

'Is he dead, Marshal Fallen?' Elmer stammered.

'No heart is strong enough to keep beating after somebody puts a bullet into it, Elmer,' Fallen drawled. 'Whoever shot Sanders, they were close. He's got powder burns.'

'That means the killer pushed his gun into him before firing, Marshal Fallen.' The deputy gulped. 'Mr Sanders probably knew his killer.'

Fallen nodded, then stepped beyond the body. He stared at the safe. Its door was wide open and there was nothing remaining inside its metal innards.

'The prize money has bin stolen,' he said.

'What we gonna do, Marshal Fallen?'

Fallen blew the lamp out and led his deputy back to the door. As he reached it the marshal withdrew the key, walked through, then closed the door behind them.

Elmer watched as Fallen inserted the key into

the lock and turned it.

'Why'd you do that, Marshal Fallen?' he asked.

Matt Fallen led his deputy back to the side door and the alley. The tall lawman paused long enough to slide the key into his shirt pocket.

'Listen up. We don't tell anyone about Sanders or the money, Elmer,' he insisted. 'Not yet anyway.'

'But why not?' the deputy asked as he and the marshal walked back towards the brightly lit street. They both paused at the corner of the Longhorn.

Fallen glanced at his young friend.

'We're buying ourselves some time, Elmer,' he said. 'Time to catch the galoot that killed Sanders and stole that small fortune in cash. Savvy?'

Elmer gripped the shotgun in his hands and nodded.

'I savvy.'

The lawmen were walking back along the busy boardwalk towards their office when they heard a volley of gunshots ring out in the distance. Matt Fallen swung round on his heels and stared in disbelief.

'Where'd them shots come from, Elmer?' he asked anxiously.

Elmer pointed to the more prosperous end of War Smoke.

'They come from over yonder, Marshal Fallen,' he answered, trying to keep hold of the hefty scattergun.

Knowing he had to find out what was happening as quickly as possible, Fallen looked over his shoulder and spotted the dead drifters' horses still tied up outside the Dixie. He called to his deputy.

'C'mon, Elmer,' he shouted. 'We'll take the two drifters' horses.'

All eyes on the crowded boardwalk watched as Fallen pulled the long leathers free of the hitching pole, stepped into the stirrup and mounted the black roan with white stockings.

Elmer looked confused. 'What in tarnation are you doing, Marshal Fallen? You can't just take other folks' horses like this.'

The marshal gathered up his reins and held the mount in check as the sound of more shots rang in their ears.

'The drifters who owned these nags are too damn dead to kick up a fuss, boy,' Fallen yelled at his junior. 'Now quit jabbering and get mounted.'

The deputy mounted the other drifter's horse,

managing to keep hold of the shotgun as he wrestled with the reins.

Both lawmen kicked their boots into the flanks
of the horses and thundered out of Front Street
to where the sound of gunshots still resounded.

SIXTEEN

The sight which greeted Marshal Fallen and his deputy as they rode up into the wealthiest part of War Smoke was one that neither of the lawmen had expected. Both riders slowed their mounts as soon as they noticed the single-horse buggy in the middle of the wide street.

Fallen pulled back on his reins as his eyes adjusted to the moonlight and his gaze fixed upon the dead body lying beside the elegant black vehicle.

The marshal dismounted the black roan and walked to where the lifeless body lay. He knelt beside the body and turned it over. He stared down at the pale face and then gazed at the group of bullet holes in the blood-soaked shirt. His mind raced as he wondered why Sanders and the banker had been shot in the chest whilst Joel Erikson and the drifters had been blasted by a scattergun.

Elmer brought his own mount to a halt beside the buggy. 'Who is it, Marshal Fallen?' he asked.

Matt Fallen rose to his feet and rubbed his jaw. 'It's Mort Heely. He's as dead as the others.'

The deputy leaned over his horse's neck and grimaced at the sight of the elderly banker.

'Who in tarnation are we looking for?' he gulped. 'Who do you figure is killing all these folks?'

'If I knew that we'd be sitting in the office drinking coffee, Elmer,' Fallen said. He swung his leg over the cantle of his saddle and poked his boot into the awaiting stirrup. 'We wouldn't be out here chasing our tails.'

Elmer pointed at the banker. 'Are we just gonna leave old Mort here, Marshal Fallen?'

'Don't fret, Elmer,' the lawman said, turning the roan. 'Mort ain't going any place. He'll still be here when Abe Sims comes to collect him.'

The star-packers rode back to the heart of War Smoke at full pace. As they reached the end of

Front Street both horsemen slowed their mounts.

The street was still filled with scores of men who were either unaware of what was happening or did not care one way or the other.

Fallen eyed every face along the wide thoroughfare as he silently led Elmer towards their office. Somewhere in War Smoke there was one merciless killer, he told himself. There might even be more than one.

As they closed the distance between themselves and the marshal's office they noticed Doc sitting on a hardback chair on the boardwalk.

'Ain't you got a bed to go to, Doc?' Fallen dismounted and looped the reins over the hitching pole.

Doc watched Elmer clamber off the back of his tall mount and then approached the marshal.

'I told Abe about the three dead bodies behind the Diamond Pin, Matt,' he said. 'He looked real happy at the news.'

Elmer stepped up on to the boardwalk. 'You best go tell him about the other two me and Marshal Fallen found, Doc.'

Fallen eyed his deputy. 'Not so damn loud, Elmer.'

Doc's face crinkled up as he looked at Fallen.

144

'You found more?'

The lawman unlocked the office door and led the way into the office.

'Just two, Doc. Just the two,' he said.

'Do I know them?' Doc poured himself a cup of the still-brewing beverage and sat himself down.

Elmer placed the hefty scattergun on the desk. 'You surely do, Doc. Sanders and Mort Heely got themselves killed.'

Matt Fallen looked at Elmer. 'You ain't quite got the knack of keeping things quiet, have you?'

'Doc don't count, Marshal Fallen.' Elmer shrugged.

Asa and Olin Fenton walked out of the shadows back into Front Street looking just like the innocent gamblers they expertly portrayed and glanced across at the still-busy saloons. Yet neither of them wanted to play cards or sample the local liquor.

'We'll catch the morning stage out of here after we've had us some shuteye, Asa,' Olin said.

'Yep, we've earned our money,' Asa said, smiling.

They were about to enter the hotel when they heard a noise down the side of the large building.

They both stopped in their tracks and saw the tall lean figure stroll out of the shadows smoking a long thin cigar.

Olin watched as the tall man in the long dust-coat stopped not ten feet from them.

'Who are you?' he asked. Asa moved to his brother's side.

'My name don't matter none,' the man said through a cloud of tobacco smoke. 'I've got a message for you, boys.'

'How'd you know the message is for us, stranger?' Asa asked the lone figure.

'The message is from Bob King,' the man drawled. 'The message is for the Fenton brothers.'

Olin nodded. 'What's the message, stranger?'

The man tilted his head back. His cold eyes sparkled like diamonds as he suddenly produced a big scattergun from beneath his long jacket.

Its barrels erupted with blinding fury and knocked both the Fenton brothers off their feet. Even before their blood-covered carcasses hit the ground the stranger had vanished into the darkness once again.

Bob King stood on the veranda of the Lucky

Dollar and watched the marshal and deputy running down the long street to where the motionless bodies lay in pools of their own gore.

The saloon owner rested his hands on the balcony rail and chuckled at the sight of the utterly bewildered lawmen as they vainly attempted to understand why so many bodies were piling up in War Smoke.

The sound of spurs behind his well-tailored shoulders made King turn and smile at his hench-man. Ty Garner looked every inch as deadly as he actually was in his long dustcoat. The lean stranger walked across King's private quarters like a phantom and stopped just shy of the veranda. He plucked the cigar from his narrow lips and flicked it out into the darkness.

'Them Fenton boys were no smarter than any of the others, King,' Garner said. 'They just stood there and ate buckshot.'

Bob King laughed and walked to where a well-sipped bottle of whiskey stood beside a dozen tumblers. 'I saw them fall, Garner. You've done your job well. Better than I could have ever imag-ined.'

'Killing's easy, King,' the gaunt figure said. 'It's staying alive that takes talent.'

King poured two glasses of whiskey. 'Did you kill Sanders?'

'Yep.' Garner nodded.

'Did you get the prize money?' King asked coyly.

Garner nodded his head slowly. 'Yep. Sanders opened the safe and then I thanked him with a bullet.'

'Where is the money?' King rubbed his anxious hands together, then lifted one of the glasses to his lips.

'Here.' Ty Garner smiled and pulled back the right side of his dustcoat. The money was still in its bag, hidden in a large pocket inside his jacket.

King grinned. 'Put it on the table and help yourself to a drink, Garner.'

Garner shook his head. 'I ain't thirsty, King.'

Bob King lowered the glass from his mouth and stared at the ghostly figure before him. A cold shiver traced his spine as he suddenly began to understand how every one of Garner's victims must have felt when finding themselves suddenly alone with the merciless killer.

It was like facing the Grim Reaper.

'Don't think I ain't beholden to you, Garner,'

King said as his mind raced, trying to find a way to appease the killer. 'I reckon we ought to split that money fifty-fifty.'

Garner shook his head. 'There ain't any call to split this money, King.'

'There ain't?' King asked.

'Nope, there ain't.' Garner suddenly pulled the still-smoking scattergun from its hiding-place and aimed it at the terrified saloon owner.

The tumbler fell from King's hand and shattered on the carpeted floor. King was shaking as he backed away from the deadly gunman.

'You can k-keep all the m-money, Garner,' he stammered as his hands instinctively rose. 'I'll make my money back buying the bank cheap from Mort Heely's kinfolk. You can ride out with all of the loot. You've earned it.'

It seemed that none of these words satisfied the lean figure with the double-barrelled weapon in his hands. Garner just stared with cold unblinking eyes at the frightened saloon owner.

'Please don't kill me, Garner,' he begged.

'It's funny,' Garner said, staring at King. 'Not one of the men you told me to kill begged for their lives like you're doing.'

'I can make you rich,' King promised.

'I'm already rich, King.' Garner smiled. 'I got the poker-game prize money in my pocket.'

The deafening sound of the twin barrels of buckshot being blasted into the saloon owner not only rocked the Lucky Dollar but resonated out into the street below.

Startled as they hovered over the bodies of the Fenton brothers, Matt Fallen and Elmer looked across the street and saw the bright flashes of venomous death dance through the open veranda windows.

'Stay down here, Elmer,' the marshal shouted over his shoulder as he bolted towards the Lucky Dollar. 'If anyone comes out of there with a smoking scattergun in his hands, shoot him.'

Elmer watched open-mouthed as the wounded marshal raced into the Lucky Dollar and headed for the wide staircase that led upstairs from the rear wall. The stunned drinkers watched as Fallen mounted the steps two at a time with his cocked Peacemaker in his hand.

The lawman reached the landing and looked towards the front of the building. Fallen knew only too well that that was where Bob King's private quarters were situated.

Fallen crossed the landing. From the corner of

his eye he could see the saloon's customers below him looking up, watching his every move.

As the tall lawman reached the closed door he tried its handle. Suddenly the entire middle of the door was blasted apart by two fresh shotgun cartridges. Debris exploded from the jagged hole in the door and knocked the unsuspecting Fallen off his feet.

Matt Fallen lay amid a million wooden splinters and choking gunsmoke. His senses were stunned as he crawled on to his knees and fired through the huge hole in the door.

As the lawman got to his feet he heard shouting coming from the street. He recognized Elmer's voice.

Fallen charged like a bull through what remained of the wooden door and narrowed his eyes against the smoke-filled air. He paused for a split second and saw the bloodstained wall and the remnants of Bob King lying on the floor.

Then he looked at the veranda and heard another barrage of lethal shotgun fire in the street. With no thought for his own safety Fallen dashed out on to the balcony. He was greeted with gunshots.

Ty Garner had looped his leg over the edge of

the veranda railings and was firing one of his six-shooters at the marshal. Fallen leapt on to the man's belly as bullets tore the side of the saloon apart. Chunks of smouldering wood rained over the veranda.

As the muscular Fallen landed on the wooden boards of the balcony he cocked and fired his Peacemaker at Garner as the lean man jumped to the ground.

Bruised and bleeding the lawman struggled back to his feet and heard another two blasts from a scattergun down below his high vantage point. Fallen reached the whitewashed railings and stared down at the man with the hefty weapon in one hand and a .45 handgun in the other.

Matt Fallen cocked the hammer of his Peacemaker and aimed the six-shooter at the merciless killer. The lawman squeezed on his trigger but its hammer fell on spent bullets.

Frantically Fallen shook the smoking casings from his gun and began plucking fresh bullets from his gunbelt. Then he saw something which chilled his heart.

His faithful deputy was lying on the sand.

'Elmer!' Fallen screamed out at his motionless

deputy but there was no response.

The dogged lawman pushed the sixth bullet into his gun and snapped its chamber shut. He then jumped from the veranda to the ground and raced through the glowing lantern light to his deputy.

As Fallen dropped to his knees beside Elmer another shot rang out in the darkness. The bullet carved a path across the shoulders of the marshal, burning a trail across his leather vest. Fallen fell on to his side and stared into his deputy's face.

'Are you OK, Elmer?' he asked.

'I'm sorry, Marshal Fallen,' Elmer said, trying to smile. 'I called out for him to stop but he kept on coming.'

Fallen placed his hand on Elmer's shoulder. 'Are you hurt bad, boy?'

'I ain't rightly sure,' Elmer told him truthfully. 'That varmint fired his scattergun from across the street. Reckon I got kinda peppered with buckshot.'

With his Peacemaker in his hand, Matt Fallen eased his aching frame up on to one elbow and narrowed his eyes. He stared down the long, smoke-filled street.

'Shoot him, Marshal Fallen,' Elmer urged. 'Shoot him.'

Fallen glanced at his deputy.

'He's gone, Elmer. He's disappeared.'

FINALE

The darkness inside the livery stable was only relieved by the glowing of the blacksmith's forge set in the far corner. Ty Garner had used every shadow to his advantage as he finally emerged into the shafts of the light cast down by the bright overhead moon. As the lean figure strode out of the blackest of cover he considered that his work was done.

He had killed every man his paymaster Bob King had instructed him to destroy. Then Garner had simply decided that he had worked far too hard to hand over the prize money he had also stolen from Doyle Sanders's office safe.

With the same cold-blooded deadliness Garner had turned his weaponry on King. The two

155

wounded lawmen were now at the other side of War Smoke and no longer posed any threat to the man with the lethal scattergun hidden under his dustcoat. As Garner made for the wide-open doors of the livery he placed a cigar between his teeth and ignited a match with his thumbnail.

All the ghostlike stranger had to do now was collect his mount and ride. There was not a man living who knew that he was the killer. Ty Garner liked it that way.

It had been so simple. It might have remained that way except for one man. As Garner inhaled the strong smoke of his cigar he noticed someone moving inside the livery. The glowing light of the forge's coals outlined a figure as it advanced.

The deadly hired gunman paused for a moment as his eyes strained to focus on the man who was coming out of the livery towards him.

For what seemed like an eternity Garner could not make out the man clearly. Then he saw him. Garner stared at the silver-haired figure who walked out into the moonlight and stopped twenty feet away from him.

'Out of my way, old-timer,' Garner instructed angrily.

Gentleman Joe Laker did not move a muscle.

He remained between the killer and the stabled horses. The renowned gambler squared up to Ty Garner and smiled. There was not a scrap of fear in either Laker's expression or his voice.

'I said get out of my way,' the ghostly gunman repeated.

'You ain't going anywhere until the marshal gets here, Garner,' Gentleman Joe said. 'Unless you intend trying to get past me.'

'I know you, Gentleman Joe.' Garner glanced over his shoulder and could hear the sound of hurried footsteps approaching. 'I ain't got the time to confab with a washed-up gambler. Now move out of my way or you'll be eating lead.'

'What's the hurry, Garner?' Laker asked. 'The whisper in town is that someone killed Sanders and stole the Longhorn prize money as well as slaughtering a lot of other folks. You ain't telling me that you did all that, are you?'

'I figured there was someone dogging my heels,' Garner said drily. 'You should have stuck to what you know, Gentleman Joe. You should have stuck to poker.'

'Doyle Sanders was a friend of mine,' Laker said. 'You shouldn't have killed him. That riled me.'

'You're a dead man,' Garner snarled, suddenly producing his big twin-barrelled shotgun from under his coat tails.

Before the huge weapon could be aimed at the gambler Gentleman Joe Laker suddenly flicked both his wrists. Two derringers appeared in the gambler's hands and were fired at exactly the same moment.

As Fallen came running round the corner into the moonlight he saw the lean killer stagger backwards as the small guns found their target. Ty Garner fell at the marshal's feet.

Matt Fallen watched as the small guns vanished back up the gambler's sleeves. The lawman looked at Garner. Two neat bullet holes in his temple wept blood as his cigar fell from his lips. Fallen reached down and pulled the moneybag from inside Garner's dustcoat.

'Reckon you found the prize money, Matt,' Laker said with a smile.

'Why'd you get involved in this, Gentleman Joe?' Fallen asked.

'I recognized Garner just after I arrived in town,' Laker replied. 'Then I discovered he killed my old friend Doyle Sanders. I figured he had stolen the money and then I worked out where he'd left his horse. All I had to do was wait.'

'Much obliged for the help, Gentleman Joe,' Fallen said. 'I don't think I could have bested that *hombre.*'

Laker stared at the moneybag. 'That ain't a very big bag of money considering how many folks died because of it, Matt.'

Both men walked into Front Street just as Doc was assisting Elmer into Fallen's office. The sound of howls came from the young deputy as Doc tended his wounds.

'Is your deputy badly wounded, Matt?'

'Nope.' Fallen grinned. 'It seems Elmer took both barrels of buckshot in his rump. Sounds like Doc has started to pluck them pellets out.'

The gambler touched his hat brim and wandered away towards the distant hotel.

Matt Fallen watched the silver-haired gambler until he disappeared from view. The lawman then walked across the moonlit street to his office. As he stepped up on the boardwalk he paused.

'See you, Gentleman Joe,' he whispered.